ALSO BY ERIC GARCIA

Casual Rex

Anonymous Rex

MATCHSTICK MEN

V VILLARD NEW YORK

MATCHSTICK MEN

A NOVEL

ERIC GARCIA

Matchstick Men is a work of fiction. The characters are entirely imaginative creations of the author, and any resemblance between these fictional characters and actual persons, living or dead, is purely coincidental.

 Published in the United States by Villard Books, a division of Random House, Inc., New York, and simultaneously in Canada by Random House of Canada Limited, Toronto.

Library of Congress Cataloging-in-Publication Data
Garcia, Eric.
Matchstick men: a novel / Eric Garcia
p. cm.
ISBN 0-375-50522-9
1. Swindlers and swindling—Fiction. 2. Obsessive-compulsive disorder—Fiction.
3. Fathers and daughters—Fiction. 4. Teenage girls—Fiction. I. Title.
PS3557.A665 M38 2002 813'.54—dc21 2002069014

Villard Books website address: www.villard.com
Printed in the United States of America on acid-free paper
98765432
First Edition
Book design by Jo Anne Metsch

For Shirley, Ethel, David, Belle, and Joe,
because I know you would have been
the proudest of all

And for Grandpa Jerry,
who taught me that at the end of the day,
laughter will always see you through

MATCHSTICK MEN

TEN

THE DINER is nearly empty this afternoon, so Roy and Frankie sit at the counter longer than usual. There's no point in bringing out the playing cards yet, not until more people show. There's an old couple in the back booth and a little family across the way, but neither set is a good pull. On a day like today, it's best to wait. This is just for fun, for practice. No need to get tricky. The deer wander into your sights when the deer wander into your sights, Roy always says. No use forcing the issue. No use shooting badgers.

The waitress, who has served Roy and Frankie almost every day for the last six years, walks by the counter and, without stopping the motion of her feet, fills both their coffee mugs to the brim. She does this fluidly, perfectly, like a ballerina, like she's been trained to do it all her life. Roy grunts his thanks. Frankie eats his burger.

"Gonna get sick off those," Roy says. The corners of his mouth are smeared with mustard.

"Off what?"

"Off them burgers. You got the gout last month, you're gonna get it again."

Frankie shrugs. His bony shoulders barely move inside the thin cotton button-down. "I got a lot I can bother you about, do I do it?"

"Sometimes," says Roy.

"You're a fat bastard, I bother you about that?"

"Sometimes."

"Am I doing it now?"

"Not saying you are. I'm saying the last time you ate a burger . . ." Roy shakes his head, wipes his thick cheeks with a paper napkin. "Fuck it, eat what you want."

"Thank you." Juice runs down Frankie's face. His grin is shot with ketchup. They eat in silence.

The waitress makes her way back across the diner, behind the counter. This time she comes to a full stop. Her name tag is a laminated sheet of paper. The ballpoint scrawl reads *Sandi.* Her hair is limp, dead across her shoulders, sunk low and heavy. Like she washed it with gasoline. "You two gonna want dessert today?" she asks.

"Nah," says Frankie.

Roy points to his coffee mug; Sandi fills it. "We're gonna sit for a while, sweetheart, if that's okay."

Sandi coughs and walks away. It's the same every day. Roy and Frankie always tip her well and treat her better than most, so she lets them sit at the counter as long as they like. She looks away when they do the things that they do. Sometimes she listens in, but mostly, she looks away.

Frankie polishes off his burger and sets to work on the garnishings, crunching whole strips of raw onion between his teeth. "That guy I told you about last week—"

"The one from the docks?"

"Yeah, he wants to get together soon. He's top-heavy, Roy, he's got people ready to take a fall—"

Roy shakes his head, takes a bite of his turkey on rye. "Not now," he mumbles. "We'll get to it later."

"Later."

"Later," Roy repeats.

Frankie spits out the unchewed onion in his mouth, leans into his partner. "What's a matter with you? Everything's later these days. You don't wanna run short, you don't wanna run long—I can't get a break. Meantime, I got guys—I got my own guys, you know—breathing down my collar, steaming me up. Can't front money if I can't make money, partner."

Turning around on the diner stool, slowly spinning the rump of his pants against the vinyl beneath, Roy fixes Frankie with his best grimace. Frankie stares back, slack skin hanging off that gaunt face, eyes sunk back like they're scared of the light. Hair cut short, buzzed to an inch, sideburns loping down the cheeks. He wants to be James Dean, but hasn't gotten there yet. Roy doubts he ever will.

"Here's the thing," begins Roy, but his words are cut off by a two-toned bell. The front door has opened, and the deer have entered the paddock.

College kids, two of them. Boy and girl, hand in hand, wearing school sweatshirts, walking toward the counter. By the time they get there, Roy and Frankie are already deeply involved in their card game, playing as if they'd been concentrating on it for the last two hours.

"That's fine, that's fine," Frankie is saying as the college kids take their seats. "I can take a beating with the rest of 'em." They are two stools down from Roy and Frankie, but two stools is nothing when it comes to the hook. Two stools is an inch.

"Hell," says Roy, folding up his cards, making a show of it, "we been playing too long at this, anyway."

"No, no, you wanna play, we can play . . ."

"Forget it," Roy says. He collects the cards laid out in front of Frankie and folds them into the deck. "You wanna see if we can get the check?"

Frankie looks around for the waitress, cranes his neck theatrically, but she's nowhere to be found. She knows better than to come around now. This is the time when she disappears for a while. This is the time when she earns her tips.

"Can you beat that?" says Roy, just a mite louder than necessary. Then, turning his body slightly to the right, he repeats the question: "Can you beat that?"

The boy, nineteen, twenty at the high end, gives off a tight little grin.

"You try to get service, you try to *pay* . . . Well, whattaya gonna do, right?"

Again, the boy grins. He's been engaged, but doesn't know it yet. Roy grins back, then turns to Frankie.

"So we wait."

"So we wait," Frankie says.

And they do. A minute, maybe two, and the waitress stays far out of their range. Soon, when the boy and girl have stopped talking to each other and sit quietly, staring at their menus, staring at the counter, Roy lays it in.

"I figured out that game," he starts.

"Which one?"

"The one, the one I showed you last week—"

A burst of laughter from Frankie, a gunshot guffaw. "Dumbest thing I ever seen."

"No, no," Roy insists, "I figured out what I was doing wrong. I figured it out, got it all working now." The deck of cards is suddenly back in his hands, fingers working over the edges.

"Look, I don't mean to belittle you or nothing," Frankie explains, "but you suck at card tricks, and I don't wanna waste my time."

"Your time's that precious?"

"Anybody's time is precious enough not to watch you pooch a card trick."

Roy sits back hard, breath coming heavy from his mouth, like he's been hit in the gut. "The hell you know," he says, recovering, pulling himself back up to the counter. "You're gonna watch, and you're gonna like it."

Frankie shakes his head, slaps the counter. Leans back, across Roy, past Roy, aiming for the boy on the other side. "Hey," he says, and just as he knew, the college kid turns his head. "Hey, you wanna see my friend make an ass outta himself?"

"Did I ask *him* if he wanted to see a card trick?" says Roy. "I asked *you*."

"And I ain't all that interested. Maybe if I got company . . ."

"Let the kid eat his lunch. He don't wanna watch a stupid—"

"Sure," says the boy, like he's in on it, like he knows he's been cued. This is how it should always go down, Roy thinks. This is heaven right here. "We'll watch."

Roy doesn't even need to suppress his grin; it fits for the time and the place, and he lets it bloom across his lips. "Thanks, kid," he says. Roy looks down at the counter, at the cards in his hand. "No room here—let's go over to that table."

Introductions are made. Roy and Frankie are Roy and Frankie, no need to cover it for this. This is their diner. This is no place for hiding. Kevin and Amanda are indeed from the local college, out on lunch break between classes.

"Nice-looking couple," says Roy once they're all seated around the laminate table. "You got kids?"

"We're—we're just dating," Kevin stammers. "Two months."

"Beautiful time," Roy tells them. "My wife and I dated for six months, then got hitched up in Vegas. Marriage is great, a blessing, gift from the Lord, but dating . . . Special time. Carefree. You kids take it slow, now. No hurry, promise me that."

Amanda smiles; she's already in. "We will," she promises. Like she's talking to an uncle. Like she's known him for life. Roy wishes they were all like Amanda. Roy knows that most of them are.

"Pick a card, my educated friend," says Roy, rifling the deck and slapping it into Kevin's outstretched palm. "Don't let me touch the deck, don't let me see the deck, just pick a card and show it to the others."

"I got a dunce cap in the car," Frankie cuts in. "You want me to get it now or wait till you're done screwing this up?"

Roy gamely ignores Frankie, shoots a hurt look toward his newfound friends, and continues. On the other side of the table, Kevin reaches into the pack and plucks out the three of clubs. He shows it to Amanda, to Frankie, to Amanda again.

"Done?" asks Roy. "Good. Put it back in the deck—don't turn it, don't turn it—just put it back wherever you want. There. Now shuffle the cards, shuffle as much as you like. Move those cards all over the place, shake up the neighborhood."

Kevin's fingers are unused to the rigors of shuffling, so the cards take a few wrong turns on the way back to the deck. Kevin laughs, Amanda laughs, Frankie laughs along. They're having fun. This is fun.

"Perfect," says Roy. "Good deck." He holds out his hand, and Kevin surrenders the cards. Roy starts dealing.

One by one, the cards flip off the top, landing faceup on the table below. "Gonna get it right," Roy mumbles, just loud enough to hear. "Gonna get it right."

Jack, eight, king, ace. Flopping onto the table, staring up at the sky. Kevin, Amanda, Frankie watching it all. Roy dealing off the top, slapping the cards down hard.

"Got this trick from an old swami lives down on Eighty-fifth Avenue," Roy says, raising one eyebrow in Kevin's direction. "You believe that?"

"I—I don't know," Kevin says.

Frankie laughs. "I know."

"Know what?"

"I know you're full of shit."

The three of clubs hits the table, and hits it hard. Kevin sees it. Amanda sees it. Frankie sees it, and does what he always does at this point. He curls his upper lip. A twinge, nothing more than a millimeter. Roy keeps flipping. Doesn't look Frankie's way, doesn't stop with the motion. He keeps on with the game, drawing cards off the top. If Roy saw the tell, there's no indication.

Roy turns to Amanda. "Do *you* believe me? About the swami?"

"I . . . I don't know you, so . . . I mean . . ." Amanda looks to Kevin, who looks back to Frankie, who smirks away. "No," she says eventually. "No, I guess I don't believe you."

Roy grins. "She's a keeper," he says to Kevin. "Forget that dating crap—marry this one today."

They laugh together for a second, for just a split second, but the chuckles join together in harmony, and Roy knows it's time. "This is it," he says, tapping the top of the deck with a meaty finger. "This is the one. Got it this time."

"You ain't got dick," says Frankie.

"Hey, hey, there's a lady present."

"All I'm saying is, you gotta practice more."

"What," says Roy, "you think I pooched this?"

Frankie shrugs and turns to Kevin, one eye on the kid and one on the faceup three of clubs. He draws a smile out of the boy, using his own tight lips as bait. Soon, they're grinning together, in this thing and on the same side. There's the card, on the table, clear as day. Roy is wrong, they all know Roy is wrong, and soon Roy will be proven wrong. It's all about the sides, Roy always says. Get 'em on your side, and no matter where you're going, the game is over before it's over.

"You wanna try this again?" asks Frankie. "We'll let ya start over."

"Screw that," mutters Roy, and now he lets some anger crawl into his voice. Just a touch, but enough to widen the gulf. Kevin's got to align with Frankie now, got to see it all from Frankie's point of view. "I got this one dead to rights."

Frankie shrugs. "Whatever you say, pal."

Roy looks to the others, trying to make some eye contact. They look away. Perfect. Roy lays it in: "Whaddaya wanna bet that the next card I turn over is the kid's card?" There it is, the phrase that pays. Laid out casually, perfectly.

"What," replies Frankie, "like a bet bet?"

"Yeah. Like a bet bet."

Frankie nudges Kevin with an elbow. "Get this guy? I'm givin' him a chance to walk away with his head up, and he wants to lose money. Hell," he says, "I'm game for that." Reaching into his pocket, pulling out a money clip. A twenty, two twenties, three twenties fall across the cards.

"Big spender," grumbles Roy. "We'll take your private jet home today." He turns to Kevin and Amanda, scooting his chair back from the table to give it a little more air, a little more space between them. "How 'bout you, kid?" asks Roy, tapping the top of the deck. "How much you wanna bet that the next card I turn over is the card you picked?"

Kevin looks again, just a quick glance down at the table to make sure that the three of clubs is really there, faceup, already dealt off the deck. No way to lose. Easy money. " 'Bout a million dollars," he laughs.

Roy lets it loose, a full-on belly laugh, wiping the corners of his eyes where real tears begin to form. "Well," he says after a time, "ol' Roy ain't got the bones to cover a bet that big. . . . Whaddaya say to a hundred?"

And somehow, some way, there's a hundred-dollar bill in Roy's hand, like it sprouted from between his fingers, a webbing of pure green. He gently lays the bill atop the table.

There is discussion between Kevin and Amanda, fiscal strategy, whispers and suggestions. Fingers digging into the pockets of their jeans, pulling out crumpled receipts and candy-bar wrappers, mixed together with loose bills and change.

"Eighty-seven dollars," Kevin announces once they've got all the money together. "It's all we've got on us."

"Fair enough," says Roy. He cracks his knuckles and picks up the deck of cards. Draws himself upright, back tight against the chair.

"Now," he says, "we just bet that the next card I flip over will be the card you picked, right?"

"Right," says Kevin, tugging at his sweatshirt, anticipating his victory, counting his found money.

"Right," says Roy.

No flourish, no fancy motions. Roy drops the deck, leans over the table, grabs the three of clubs between his fingers, and flips it over. Facedown. He scoops the money off the table and into his pocket, and follows the passing waitress back to the lunch counter.

"Check, please," he tells her. "We're ready to head out."

||||||||

ROY IS driving. Frankie relaxes. They're in Roy's Chevy Caprice, just past ten years old. It's black, with windows tinted down to the legal limits and a dark gray interior. The wax job is rubbing out, but the vinyl is taut and the floor mats are spotless. Roy could buy a new car, he knows, buy a hundred new cars if he wanted, but the Chevy doesn't attract attention, the engine runs fine, the carpets are clean, and it gets him where he wants to go.

Inside the car, after the diner, Frankie is elated. They've scored bigger than this; they always score bigger than this. But any score is a happy score for Frankie. He rifles through the bills like a schoolboy with trading cards. Roy drives, his fingers tight around the steering wheel, red blooms spreading out from the knuckles. The pressure is there, in his head. Pushing.

"You see them slink outta there?" Frankie giggles. "Back to school, kids . . ."

"Timing was off."

"We did good. A hundred bucks—well, eighty-seven, but—"

"Coulda done better."

"That's all they had. Took all they had."

"And we coulda done better with the timing," Roy says.

Frankie gives up. He nods. "Five years we been doing that gag, you'd think we'd have it down by now."

"You'd think."

Frankie leans back in his seat, puts his feet up on the dash. His black boots are filthy, the soles scuffing up the glove compartment. "Get your fucking feet down," Roy barks, knocking Frankie's legs off with a hearty swipe.

"So, wait—wait—I'm supposed to say, 'You suck at card tricks—' "

"Card *game,*" says Roy. "*Game.* That's it, right there—that's the problem. Trick, that's a giveaway. Trick, a spin, a screw-around. Trick is the trick. Now *game* . . . shit, game's a walk, a pleasant afternoon in the park. No one puts up walls for a game."

"So you're saying it's all words."

Roy shakes his head. "Not all words, no, but they send out the wrong message if you use 'em wrong. Look, all I'm saying is that you have to be careful. You go out to hunt a few deer, do you need a bazooka?"

"How big are the deer?"

"No, you don't need a bazooka. And a potato gun ain't gonna help you, either. You wanna shoot deer, you need a rifle. Same thing with marks, right? You gotta pick the weapon, and pick it right, or you're gonna either blow it outta the water or come up way short of the target."

"And *game* is the right weapon?" Frankie asks.

"In this case, yeah. *Game* is where you wanna be with that."

Frankie takes a moment to think it over. Puts his feet back on the dashboard, has them batted down again a moment later. Roy doesn't tolerate a filthy automobile. He's seen what Frankie does to his series of cars. Empty soda cans in front, empty condom wrappers in back. Food crumbs, crumpled maps. A movable war zone. Disgusting. The kind of thing that can happen to any car, if you don't watch out for it. If you're not vigilant. Roy is vigilant. Roy is super-vigilant when it comes to Frankie. Ever since Hank died, Frankie's been a good guy and a great partner, but his filth is a virus.

"There's a diner out on Fourth Street," Frankie begins. "Might be a good stop."

"Not hungry."

"Me neither. But we could order up some fries, try the game again. Practice."

"Not today."

"I think we could nail it—"

"Not today."

Roy takes the corner hard, legs braced against the floor as the tires skitter across the pavement. Frankie goes with the motion, letting his shoulder rest up against the Caprice's door, the handle digging into his side.

"Look," says Frankie after a while, "I don't wanna get on you about this—"

"Then don't."

"—but you wake up at eleven, call me out to lunch, we run a stupid little game on some kids, and then you wanna knock off for the day?"

"Did I say that?" asks Roy. "Did I say we were done for the day?"

"Are we?"

"No. I'm tired, that's all."

"You're always tired. Last three weeks, you been sleepwalking through every job." Frankie waits a moment, like he's not sure whether or not to continue. "You still taking your pills?"

"Partner," grumbles Roy, "get your goddamned feet off my dashboard."

There's nothing else to say. Roy drives on. Frankie flips on the radio, finds one of his stations. Golden oldies. Crooners. A guy his age, listening to music made for his parents. He sings along with some has-been Vegas lounge act.

In the backseat, there's a newspaper, folded neatly into thirds. As they cross over a set of worn-out railroad tracks, Roy reaches back, grabs the paper by the left corner, and heaves it into Frankie's lap. "You wanna run a roofing job?"

Frankie brightens. "No kiddin'?"

"Section D. Get a good one."

"How old's the paper?"

"Two weeks. Long enough for family to clear out."

Frankie tears into the newspaper with relish, tossing the pages about the car. Roy holds back a grimace. Bile tickling his throat. No point in telling him to pick the trash up, no point in getting into an argument now. He's a good partner, a good partner, a good partner. It used to be that it didn't bother him at all, these things Frankie did, these little personality quirks. The casual disregard for tidiness. The flashy clothes. The loud music. Used to be that they were endearing, or they were tolerable.

Last few weeks, since the doctor moved away, it's been different. Like there's an ocean of resentment out there, a tossing sea of anger. Bloodred waves. Wade on in, they call, wade on in. Roy feels like he's been toeing up to the line, testing the waters. Edging away at the last moment. Doc woulda liked to know about it. That's the kinda thing he would have written down, talked about for weeks. But the doc moved away. That's what they all do, eventually. They move away.

"I got an Isaacson over on Twenty-third Court," Frankie says, finger running beneath an obituary title. "Eighty-three, survived by a wife and daughter."

"Daughter's no good. She could be there."

"And if she is, we blow it off. You always said there's no use in being scared by the henhouse—"

"—if the fox is eating his dinner, yeah, yeah, I know what I said." Roy sighs. He can't believe the things he hears about himself. Sometimes these days, he thinks he'd like to find the old Roy in an alleyway, beat the shit out of him. Slit his throat. Sometimes.

"Isaacson?"

"Twenty-third Court."

"We could drop by Vic's place and pick up the van," Roy suggests. Now he's thinking, now he's planning, and the other thoughts retreat. Fall back into the shadows, waiting. Better this way. Safer.

"And the outfits," Frankie adds. He's turning it on, getting excited. "C'mon, let's do it. Thirty-minute job, tops."

MRS. ISAACSON has just gotten off the phone with her daughter when the roofing truck pulls up outside her suburban home. She and Linda have made plans to go to the Salvation Army this afternoon and give away some of Hal's old things, the clothes he never really liked, the ties he never really wore. Hal was always a great supporter of charity, but now he's gone, and Mrs. Isaacson wants to fulfill what she believes would have been his last wishes. No time for that. Heart attack. Gone in his sleep. Didn't feel a thing, the doctors said. Last wishes in his dreams.

She doesn't know why they're ringing her bell, but Mrs. Isaacson opens the door for the two gentlemen dressed in light gray outfits, coveralls splattered with paint and tar. One very thin, one heading to fat, they stand in her doorway like the number 10, smiling, holding clipboards.

"Afternoon, ma'am," says the heavy one. His brow is sweaty, skin tanned. "Jonas Taylor, Associated Air and Roof. Is Mr. Isaacson at home? Your father, perhaps?"

Mrs. Isaacson drops her eyes. Her voice is thin, weak. "My husband . . ."

"I see," says the man. "He didn't tell me he had such a pretty wife. Well, that's fine, that's fine, either one of you can sign off for this—"

"We wanted to get started early," says the other one, the thin one, the man with the long sideburns and longer face. "On account of the rain and all . . ."

"No, no," says Mrs. Isaacson. "My husband—Hal—he passed away . . ."

The heavy one takes a step back. "Oh," he says, short, clipped. "Oh."

"A heart attack," she continues.

"Oh," he repeats. The man rubs his chest absentmindedly, as if he were feeling Hal's past pain. "I am . . . I am so sorry, ma'am."

She nods. "It was two weeks ago. Are you . . . friends of his?"

"No, ma'am," says the skinny one. "We were just hired by him to do some work for the house—there was a roof problem. . . . Look, we'll get outta your way. You don't need this now."

The men share a quick look, and the big one doffs his hat. "Ma'am," he says, bowing slightly at the waist. "I am powerfully sorry at your loss."

Mrs. Isaacson hasn't seen a man like this in sixty years, a kind, polite man who tips his hat at a woman and calls her ma'am, not since her and Hal's courting days. Nowadays, all the servicemen are hoodlums or thieves or just plain rude. Nowadays, she prefers to stay indoors and do her shopping over the phone than deal with service people.

As the two men head back down the front walk toward their van, Mrs. Isaacson calls out, "What did my husband hire you to do?"

"Just a roof job, ma'am" is the reply. Their backs are turned; she doesn't know which one is speaking. "Repair some damage before the rainy season. You should get it looked at sometime."

"Wait," she calls out. They stop. "If you were going to do it anyway . . . Hal always handled the money, the house. . . . But if you were going to do it anyway—"

They're back at the doorstep, rifling through the clipboard, talking to each other, working out figures and numbers and talking about tar and shingles and time. "It's an eighteen-hundred-dollar job," says the older one, the chubby one. "About three hours, all told. Not long, but I wouldn't want to be in your hair . . ."

"Not at all," Mrs. Isaacson tells the men. "I was just going out to meet my daughter for a few hours."

"Tell you what, then," says the younger man. "We'll go back to the warehouse, pick up the shingles, come on back, and get started right away. By the time you get home, you'll have a brand-new roof, we'll be gone, it'll be like we were never here. No muss, no fuss."

"Yes . . ." says Mrs. Isaacson, glad that Hal took care of this for her before he left. Glad that he contacted these nice men. She hopes that he thought ahead on other matters, too. "Yes, that will be good."

"We should probably get a deposit," says the thin one. "Just so our boss—"

"Forget the deposit," says the partner. "I'm sure Mrs. Isaacson is good for it." He tips his hat again and smiles warmly, and she wonders if she should bring them tea or cookies or something while they work.

But the little one is agitated. "Remember last time? Mr. Yarrow hit the roof when we forgot the deposit—"

"It's fine, it's fine, she's good for it—"

"I'm sure she is, but it's Mr. Yarrow I'm worried about—"

Mrs. Isaacson doesn't like to see these two men argue with each other. "Gentlemen," she cuts in, coming between them, placing a thin, wizened hand out to attract their attention. "I thank you for your trust, but rules are rules. I'd be happy to give you a deposit."

"Ma'am, you don't have to—"

"Posh. You shouldn't get in trouble over me. Now, would cash be all right with you two?"

"Bless your heart," says the heavy one, tipping his hat one final time, "cash is just peachy, ma'am."

||||||||

"TWELVE HUNDRED bucks," Frankie says. He's got the money tight inside a rubber band, the hundreds rolled up into a cylinder. "Sweet the way you set up the blow-off."

Roy turns onto the highway. He doesn't want to be on the streets anymore. Mrs. Isaacson gave them juice in boxes for the trip they were supposed to take back to the warehouse. They were for her grandson, she said, but he stopped drinking apple juice when he turned seven. She still has cartons of it in the house. Roy sips at the drink. It tastes bitter going down, scratching at his throat.

"Funny thing is," Frankie is saying, "I think that broad had a real roof problem. My uncle used to be a roofer, and I went with him on a few jobs when I was back in school. Couldn't see much from down where we was, but the sides of them shingles looked worn through. She gets that up top, gonna have a whole lotta water gardens inside that house come rainy season."

Roy takes another sip. The cars on either side of him are zipping by, blurs of red and green blasting past his vision. The Chevy rumbles along. The speedometer reads sixty, but he might as well be on a bicycle.

"Must be doin' ninety," he mumbles.

"Whazzat?" asks Frankie, already engrossed in the obituaries once again.

"Said they must be doing ninety. These other cars."

"Ninety," says Frankie, mocking Roy's deep tones. "Sure, Roy, they're doing ninety. Hey, here's one." He folds the paper back, accidentally tearing the corner of the paper, the edge ripping off and fluttering to the ground. The noise is impossibly loud in Roy's ears, like a jet taking off two feet away. But the ripping and the tearing are nothing in comparison to the sound of the paper shred floating to the floor of the car—wings, flapping at Roy's eardrums, pounding on them—landing with an explosion, like someone dropped a bowling ball through a glass factory. Roy's hand tight on the wheel, red knuckles turning white, grasping the vinyl, twisting it. Teeth clenched, jaw tight, holding back the vomit, the rush of food and acid boiling up through his throat, ready to explode, to crush his jaw with the noise and the pain—

". . . and he was a diamond broker." Frankie's voice, cutting through the noise. Everything is quiet again. Except for Frankie. The feeling is gone.

"Who is?" asks Roy. The other cars have slowed down. The Caprice keeps pace.

"The next stop. The guy. He was a diamond broker. Died from a stroke, no kids, just the wife. Way I figure it, they've got a lot of bucks, probably in cash. We can pull off a bigger number this time, I'm thinking. Maybe a few grand—"

"I'm tired," Roy says. "I'm going home."

"Aw, c'mon, we're on a roll—"

"I'm going home."

Frankie tries to argue, but Roy doesn't answer. For every point that Frankie makes, Roy drives another silent mile. It's a lopsided battle, and it's over before it started.

Frankie's apartment building is all glass and steel, a modern monument Roy doesn't understand. Once, he asked Frankie what it cost him to live there, and when Frankie told him the rent, Roy didn't know whether to hit his partner upside the head or cry alongside him. He tried to explain to Frankie about investing, about putting money away. About buying a place instead of renting when you could afford it. But Frankie and Roy are Frankie and Roy, and their nights are as different as their days are similar. Frankie buys a new car every six months. Frankie buys a new ladyfriend every two. Frankie is always looking for the next score, because Frankie is always in debt.

"You give me a call tomorrow morning," he says to Roy as he climbs out of the Caprice. "I got a lot set up for us."

"We'll see," says Roy. "I'm real tired, I gotta rest."

Frankie stops, steps back. Concerned. "Don't do this to me," he says. "There's a club down south we can pick off with the zoo gag. Maybe five grand."

"We'll see."

Frankie leans in the open window of the car; his hair brushes against the roof, pulls back the skin on his sloping forehead. His sunken eyes bug out. "I got guys I gotta pay off, okay? I don't like to admit that, but I got these guys."

"So you want a loan?"

"I want a *score*. Look, just call me, okay?"

"Sure," says Roy. "I'm tired, that's all."

"And do me a favor, partner—take your fucking pills."

Roy doesn't wait around anymore after that. The Caprice can still move fast when it has to.

||||||||

SIX YEARS ago, Roy bought this house. The neighborhood is nice. Nothing too fancy, but steady. Staying in place. Holding value. The yard is well maintained, the surrounding homes are kept up, and no one bothers anyone else. No one cares. Perfect. The house itself is not large, only three bedrooms and two baths, but there's just Roy and only Roy, so it's bigger than he needs. One of the bedrooms is a bedroom. The second bedroom is an office. One chair, one desk, one lamp. It's where Roy keeps his records, his files. Where he writes his letters. The third bedroom, the back bedroom, is currently in use as a den, though no one but Roy ever goes inside. There is a couch in there that folds out into a bed, an old black-and-white television set with bent rabbit ears, and, in the corner, a dressing table and bureau with nothing inside. The walls are covered with art purchased at hotel-suite sales, twenty-dollar watercolors meant to keep the room trashy. Ugly. Uninteresting.

Off to the far side of the room, next to the empty bureau, there is a ceramic horse, four feet high at the shoulder and just about as long. It is blue and yellow. Knotted piping runs up and down the sides, spiraling decorations with chipped paint. The horse's eyes are a dulled, muted black. It stares blankly at the television all day long. Around its neck is a hardened rope, stuck there as if a real horse were turned into ceramic just seconds before being dragged into servitude. The rope is yellow, the paint matching with the rest of the statue. This is the way Roy likes it.

The den is his first stop when he arrives home. It always is, at least when he's got cash on him, which is nearly every trip. Most days, Roy comes inside, throws his jacket on the hook, and walks right into the back bedroom. But these days, since the doc left town, there are extra steps.

First, Roy steps inside his house and closes the door behind him. He turns the deadbolt, locking it up tight. Then he unlocks it and turns it again. Unlocks it and turns it again. Unlocks it and turns it again. Four times, and now it's locked. No doubt about it. Little doubt about it.

He places his jacket on the hook by the door, then moves it down a peg. Up a peg. Down a peg. No way to know if the first one was sturdy enough. Searches through the pockets to make sure he hasn't missed any cash, then searches again for good measure. Yesterday, he searched a third time just to be sure and found a twenty-dollar bill hiding among the folds of cloth. Today he searches a third time, and though he doesn't find anything, he thinks it might be a good idea to add this third search to his daily regimen, just in case.

By the time he reaches the den, Roy has already placed his shoes back inside their shoe boxes on the third shelf of his closet, and wiped his socks on the tile a few extra times. Might be residual dirt to scuff up the carpet. He steps through the door, skirts the couch, and attends to the horse.

The ceramic head is heavy in Roy's arms as he slides it up and off the body. Rests it on the floor below, taking pains to balance it just right. Roy reaches into his pockets and pulls out the day's take.

After splits with Frankie, Roy's got almost seven hundred dollars in cash. Small but easy haul, an hour's work at tops. He prepares to reach down into the statue, through the horse's neck, in order to gingerly place the rolled-up money atop the stacks already inside, but there's no need to go through that. The cash is piled up to the brim, the ceramic statue nearly overflowing with bills of all denominations. That happened quickly.

It is probably time to take another trip to the Caymans, Roy thinks. The last time the horse got this full, he was eighty-nine thousand over the amount he allowed himself to keep in the house. The *safe amount.* The *cash allowance.*

But the beach and the sun and the noise of the islands are too much for him to contemplate right now. The world is too bright down there. Not now, but soon. It can wait a spell. It will have to wait. Now all Roy wants to do is put the horse's head back where it belongs and crawl into bed. To sleep until the sounds and the pressure and the pain go away. To wake up and find out that Doc Mancuso has moved back to town and is happy to supply him with the soft pink pills once again. To cover his head with the blanket, tuck his knees under his chin, grab a handful of hair in each fist, and blot out the sun.

NINE

FRANKIE IS banging on the door. Roy can see him from the den, make out his weaselly features through the thin sheets hanging over the front windows. He's only got one eye open, but he can see Frankie standing on the stoop. Pounding with his little fists. Kicking out with those little feet. Roy would laugh, but he's worried he might throw up if he laughs. That's a new one. Two days old now. He was lying down in the recliner, head back, eating a can of tuna, and he thought, *What would it be like if I throw up now? Would I choke on my own vomit? Would anyone find me before I died?* Since then, it hasn't been far off his mind.

"Roy, goddammit!" Frankie is yelling, his voice muted through the wooden front door. "I know you're in there!"

Roy doesn't believe that Frankie really knows he's in the house. Frankie bluffs, but he's bad at it. Roy taught Frankie how to bluff, long ago, but Frankie didn't want to learn about the tells. How to hide 'em, how to spot 'em. He just wanted to go right on bluffing his way through everything. Frankie needs Roy for the cover. Roy knows it.

"I'll call the cops, I'll do it," threatens Frankie. He pounds a few more times. "I'll put all my shit where they can't find it, I'll call them and they'll come down here and—well, hell, I'll call them, that's all I'm saying."

Roy knows Frankie would never do such a thing. He hates the cops. Paranoid about them. Thinks they have scanners, ways of knowing if you're lying to them. Frankie can't be on the same street as a cop. But the mere threat makes Roy move. For Frankie to even threaten that . . . To call the police. The police. To have to *talk* to them, to *speak* with them . . . Moving slowly, deliberately, being careful not to scuff the carpet, Roy lifts himself off the recliner and shuffles to the front door. He keeps the latch on tight as he releases the deadbolt and pulls at the knob.

Frankie's nose pops through the opening, lips following. "Jesus, Roy, you had me scared. Open up, lemme in."

"Take off your shoes," says Roy.

"What? Why?"

"Dirt. Take 'em off, or you don't come in."

"You gotta be kidding me. C'mon, it's me, open up."

"Boots. Off."

Frankie pulls his nose back, sticks an eye in its place. Scans what he can see—the living room, part of the dining room, Roy, the eyeball dancing up and down as it soaks in the picture. Frankie steps back. "You stopped taking the pills, didn't you?"

"Are you taking off your shoes or am I closing the door again?"

Roy can hear muttering from behind the door as Frankie struggles with his boots. He wants to laugh again, but stops just short as he feels the bile rising in his throat. He doesn't want to vomit. Not here, not on the carpet.

Frankie comes in holding his boots. His socks have holes in

them. Thousand-dollar boots and forty-two-cent socks. That's Frankie. He's got doughnuts in the other hand. "Breakfast of champions," he says. Tosses them on the kitchen table. He looks around the place, walks through the living room.

"Looking for something?" asks Roy.

"My partner. You seen him?"

Roy falls back into his recliner. "Came all this way to make jokes?"

"I been calling for five days, a guy gets worried."

"I go places. I go outta town."

Frankie shakes his head. "Not this time, you didn't. You been right here, I can see your lumpy ass print on the couch."

Roy shrugs. "Been busy."

Boots still in one hand, Frankie crosses the room and pulls open the front window shades. Sunlight streams in, slapping Roy's face. He winces, covers his eyes with a thick forearm.

"What're you," Frankie says, "a goddamned bat?"

"You're very loud."

"That's just 'cause you ain't heard normal speech in a week. This is what real people sound like, Roy. Real people in the outside world."

"You're still very loud."

Frankie looks at his partner hard. Roy glares back. "You take your pills?" he asks Roy.

"Fuck off."

"Did you take your pills?"

"I answered you already. I said fuck off."

By way of answer, Frankie throws his boots on the carpet, dirty side down. Before they've even hit the fibers, before they've made a mark, Roy is out of the chair. On his knees by the door, grunting, grabbing for the boots. Holding them aloft, away from the carpet. Inspecting for dirt, for a stain. His fingers probe every strand, searching for filth and grime.

Frankie is down next to him, hand on his partner's back. Roy feels like he's going to vomit right here, right on the carpet. The stain will never come out. The thought makes him gag, stings his throat.

"What happened to Dr. Mancuso?" Frankie asks, his voice low. Kind.

Roy can't get it out. His throat is closed. The noises coming out are tight coughs, clipped breaths. Frankie sits on the floor, grabs his partner's head. Takes the boots away, shows Roy the clean carpet. Looks in his eyes.

"It's okay," he says. "You're okay. Tell me what happened to Doc Mancuso."

Roy takes a breath. It goes down hard. "He left," Roy says. Panting.

"Left the practice?"

"Left town. He left town."

Frankie nods. "He go far?"

"Chicago." Easier now. Air coming through.

"Far enough. When?"

Roy thinks back. "Eight weeks ago. Give or take."

"Jesus, Roy . . ." Frankie stands, pulling Roy to his feet. One hand beneath the bigger man's armpit, trying to help him balance as they rise. "So you been outta pills for how long?"

Roy isn't sure anymore. He stopped counting a while ago. "A month, maybe."

"So we gotta get you a new doc, that's all."

Roy shakes his head. The motion makes him dizzy. "Doc Mancuso—"

"—isn't around anymore. I know you got along good with him, but that's . . . that's not an option anymore. We can't—you can't do this. You gotta be well. You gotta function. We got jobs to do."

"You do 'em," says Roy, turning away.

"*We* do 'em. You still run this thing. Might not look like it now, but you're tops of the pops. Two-man operation, pal."

Roy can't think about running games. He can only think about getting back in his recliner. Sitting down. Safe there. He stands, shuffles across the room.

"Okay," Frankie says after some thought, "I know a guy."

"A guy."

"A doctor. Good guy."

"Diverter?" Roy asks.

Frankie stands, shakes his head. "Nah, he's a straight arrow. He's the guy I took my ma to when she was having them visions."

"I'm not having visions—"

"Not saying you are. But he's a shrink like any other shrink, and he can give you the pills you need."

Roy doesn't want to argue. Arguing means talking. Talking means saliva. Saliva means bile, and bile means vomit. He nods instead.

"Go take a shower," Frankie insists. "I'll make a few phone calls, see what I can set up."

On his way into the bathroom, Roy turns around and finds his partner on the phone. "Frankie," he says.

"Yeah?"

"You wipe that thing down when you're done with it?"

"Go take that shower, Roy."

ROY SITS in the passenger side of Frankie's new sports car, wedged into the leather bucket seat. The options alone cost more than Roy's entire Caprice. The music blasting over the premium sound system is loud but tolerable. Old standards. Ella scatting at eighty decibels.

"Secretary said there ain't a lot of crap to fill out," Frankie tells Roy as they pull into the parking lot. "But we gotta get there a few minutes early."

"You give my real name?"

"Yeah, sure. You're the real you, ain't ya?"

Fourth floor, suite 413. Dr. Harris Klein and Associates. Inside the sparse, white-walled lobby, Roy fills out a series of forms. Name, address, medical history. Under occupation, he writes "Antiques Dealer." This is the standard front. There are enough ugly pieces of art in his home to qualify for the distinction.

"You want me to go in with you?" Frankie asks.

"What're you, my mother?"

"Just asking. I'll stick out here. Read some of these magazines."

When they call Roy in a few minutes later, he hands his forms to the secretary and makes his way down a short, wood-paneled hallway. A door at the end is open. He pauses.

"Come in," he hears a voice call out. "Come inside, please."

Dr. Klein waits for Roy inside his office, standing in front of a thick mahogany desk. He's short, thin. Hairy. Curly mop up top, glasses perched on the pert nose. Dress shirt, slacks, no jacket. Rolex on the right wrist. Slight bulge in back pocket where his wallet would be. Roy decides not to pickpocket the doctor. Degrees and plaques line the walls, interspersed with family photos and whimsical caricatures. The carpet is a dark, fruity red, like it's been soaked in wine.

"How do you find stains?" Roy asks.

The doctor is confused. "I'm sorry?"

"On the carpet. It's so dark. How do you find the stains?"

Dr. Klein grins and holds out his hand for Roy to shake. "I don't worry about that much," he says. "We don't have a lot of food in here."

Roy wants to tell him that it's not just food. Stains can come from anywhere. Bleach. Blood. Urine. But he maintains. Shakes the doctor's hand. Takes a seat like he knows he should.

Dr. Klein sits down across from Roy, turning a chair to face his new patient. "I'm glad you came today, Roy. I understand your old therapist moved away."

"Wasn't a therapist," Roy mutters. "Just my shrink."

"It's about the same thing, isn't it?"

"No. Doc Mancuso gave me my pills. That's the end of it."

"I see," says Dr. Klein. "So you didn't talk things over with him."

"Like what?"

"Like . . . your problems, your thoughts. Trying to get to the heart of things."

Roy sighs, leans into the chair. "My partner—my buddy Frankie—he said he knew you, said I could come to you, and you could get me the pills I need. Doc Mancuso had me on a hundred and fifty milligrams of Anafranil and seventy-five of Zoloft. If you can't do that, this session's over before it's fucking started."

Klein smiles. "You certainly get right to the point."

"And you skirt it. Can you get me the pills or not?"

"Yes," says the doctor.

Roy relaxes. "Then let's get that prescription pad out."

"I tell you, Roy, I don't usually prescribe medicine until I've had a little chat with the patient first."

"How long's that take?"

"You've got somewhere else to be?"

"I've always got somewhere else to be." Roy's feeling good now, not worrying about the carpet as much. Not worrying about the vomit. Much. He'll be getting the pills soon, and that helps.

"A few minutes of your time, then. I'll keep it short."

"Good," says Roy. He sits back in the chair. It's comfortable. Padded. Like the recliner at home. "You wanna talk about my mother?"

"Do you?"

"No, but that's how Doc Mancuso started things out. My mother, my father, my sisters."

"Are you close with them?"

"They're dead. All of 'em. You give me a family member, I'll tell you they're dead."

Dr. Klein shuffles in his seat. "That's—that's not necessary." He picks up the thin file folder on his desk, runs a finger down the side. "Says here you're an antiques dealer." Roy nods. "Do you enjoy that line of work?"

" 'Sokay."

"Business good?"

"Up days and down days."

"You know," Dr. Klein begins, stepping out of the chair, "I bought this piece a few years back at an estate sale. Chippendale, they told me, but I think I may have been—what's the term?—snookered. Can you tell if it's—"

"I'm off the clock, doc. Can we get on with this?"

Klein sits back down. "Fine," he says. Upset, maybe? Roy can't read him. "Married?"

"I was."

"What was her name?"

"Heather."

"And you're . . . divorced?"

"Brilliant," says Roy.

"Any kids?"

Roy shrugs. The doctor repeats his question. "Maybe," Roy answers.

Klein raises an eyebrow. "Maybe. Maybe. That's a new one."

"Glad to help."

"Maybe as in they might be yours, maybe as in . . . ?"

Roy had to go through this with Doc Mancuso, but that man knew when to drop an issue. "Maybe as in she was pregnant when she left me. So maybe I got a kid, maybe I don't."

"You haven't seen them."

"What am I saying here? Yeah, I haven't seen them."

The doctor nods. Writes something down. "Have you tried?" he asks.

"Have I—what do you care?"

"I'm just trying to get to know you better. Get some sense—"

"What's the point in trying if—Look, look, my wife left me on a Tuesday morning, divorce papers sent through the mail. For all I know, she got hit by a crosstown bus that night. For all I know, there ain't no kid to see. End of story. Get on with the drugs."

Dr. Klein seems to understand. He sits back in his chair, looks at the file. "You say you've got some obsessive-compulsive behavior, coupled with depression."

"That's why he had me on the pills. Doc Mancuso, that's what he said it was. That's why the Anafranil and the—"

"I know, I understand. It's just hard for me to make a diagnosis and dispense medication to a patient without getting a full grasp of—"

Roy scootches forward; the chair drags furrows in the dark red carpeting. He's a foot away from the doctor, eyes locked. He stands. Places his hands over the doctor's hands, locking them in place. Strapped down. Klein doesn't struggle. "I spent the last week of my life in my living room recliner," Roy says, his breath heavy, fogging the doctor's glasses. "Watching the carpet. Watching the fibers on the goddamned carpet. Now I know this ain't normal, but I can't do a thing about it. When I try to leave my house, I can't, because I don't know if I turned off the burners. So I check them to make sure they're not hot, and then I get ready to leave, but suddenly I'm thinking, uh-oh, what if when I was checking them the last time, I accidentally flipped one of them on? And even if I manage to get out of the door, I can't leave the front step, 'cause I don't know if I locked the door right, and I don't know if I shut all the windows. So I stay inside and go through my routines and the whole time I'm doing that, I'm worrying that I'm gonna vomit. And the whole time I'm worrying that I'm gonna vomit, that there's nothing that can stop me from letting loose right there and then, I'm thinking at the same time that I'm a grown adult, that I should know what the hell is going on inside my own mind, and the more I think about it the more I realize I should just blow my fucking head off, and the more I want to blow my fucking head off, the more I think about what that's going to do to the goddamned carpet.

"And that's a good day, doc. So gimme the fucking pills and let me get on with my life."

||||||||

ROY WASHES down the medicine with a swig of soda. One little green pill, that's all it takes. New medication, Doc Klein said, a better class of drug. Effexor, something like that. One pill takes care of the OCD and the depression. New inhibitors, he said. Anafranil is out. Zoloft is out. Roy doesn't care. He's glad to take anything.

"He just gave 'em to you?" Frankie is saying. "At the office?"

Roy nods. "Said the pharmacy would have to special-order it, said it would take a few days. He gave me a week's worth."

"That's it?"

"Said he wants me to come back," says Roy. "To talk. Nice fucking shrink you put me on."

"Hey, he's a good guy."

"He's a real chatterbox, wants to talk for an hour."

Frankie steers his car into the parking lot of a small convenience store. "There's other guys in town."

"Other guys'll make me talk for *two* hours. Fuck it, I'll go, I'll go."

As they walk through the convenience store, Roy can already feel the medicine starting to work inside his body. Knows it's not possible. Doesn't care. He hasn't thought about the bile in his throat for ten minutes. No carpet in the store to worry about. Linoleum, scuffed. Dirty. That puts him out a little. Best to think about other things.

Frankie moves through the aisles, pulling down the worst that the food industry has to offer. Chips. Doughnuts. All the things that should kill him in time, but probably won't. Roy doesn't understand how Frankie stays so thin. Doesn't particularly care, so long as he cleans up after himself. Frankie feels about food the way he feels about money: It's there to be consumed, so what's with all the worry?

When the store is cleared out, they approach the cashier. Behind the counter is a lottery board announcing the available games and the previous day's winning numbers. "Gimme one of them pick fives," Roy says. He pays a dollar and marks off the ticket with the exact same numbers that won the day before. "I want to play this for the drawing on the twenty-second."

"Sir," says the clerk, noticing the ticket, "the odds of the lottery hitting the same numbers in the same month—the same numbers ever—they are astronomical."

"You my financial advisor?"

"No, sir—"

"You my mother?"

"No, sir—"

"No, sir, you are not. So take your dollar, gimme a ticket for the twenty-second, and clean up this joint before I report you to the board of health."

Roy can't believe what's happened to customer service these days.

BACK IN the car, on the drive over to the Laundromat, Frankie starts in. "I talked to Saif again, he still wants to meet up."

"Who?"

"Saif," says Frankie. "Saif, the guy from the docks."

"What is he, an Arab?"

"Or something. I think he's from Turkey."

Roy examines the lottery ticket, crumples it between his fingers. Scratches up the date, wears out the first number, so the ticket looks like it's for the second instead of the twenty-second. Puts it on the floor of the car, steps on it. Gets it dirty. Used. "And he's looking to . . ."

"Art. Fakes. He wants to unload some stuff."

"Whadda we know about that?" Roy asks.

"Let's just meet with the guy."

"For what?"

"To meet with him. To make nice." Frankie rips open a bag of potato chips and shoves a handful into his mouth. "Jesus, Roy, you don't budge."

The Laundromat is across the street. Roy sits up in the car seat, straightens his shirt. Tucks the lottery ticket back in his pocket. "We'll discuss it later."

"It's always later—"

"Task at hand," Roy says. "Focus."

"Can I get a maybe outta you? A single fucking maybe?"

Roy knows this will be easier if he just gives in. Over in a second, no more conversation. It's always this way with Frankie. That makes Roy want to stand his ground even more, but there's a job to be done. "Maybe. Drop me off on the corner."

Frankie pulls over, and Roy steps out of the car. He considers putting on a tie, then drops the idea. White collar, but not too white collar. That's the look. Frankie pops his trunk, and Roy grabs the clothes inside. They're clean, but they could be cleaner. Either way, they're getting washed today.

The sun is out, and the rays beat down on Roy's face. It was supposed to be cool this week. Roy doesn't like the heat. He doesn't like to sweat. Even if it's not a tell, he doesn't like to sweat. Maybe it helps the part, though. Maybe today it's not so bad.

The Laundromat has big fans blowing the hot air in circles, enough to cool it down a notch. Make it bearable. Small place, maybe twenty washers, ten oversized dryers. Not too crowded, either.

A single man, a black man, sitting on a washer, reading through a magazine. Not what Roy wants.

A couple, laughing, foreheads together, noses touching. Kissing. Not what Roy wants, either.

At the end of the aisle, a middle-aged woman separates whites from colors. There are shirts in there, women's blouses, but there are also small cotton undies. She has kids. The jewelry is minimal, but what there is seems average enough from a distance. Clothing is discount rack, but put together with a degree of care. Bleached blonde. Eyebrows still black. This is what Roy is looking for. This is the place to be.

Roy drags himself down the left aisle, looking at the washers, searching for a good one to use. He's humming beneath his breath, a happy tune. Nothing concrete, just happy. A set of washers two down from the woman with the kid's clothes is open, lids gaping wide.

"These taken?" Roy asks.

"No," says the woman. Her voice is low, scratchy. She yells a lot, Roy figures.

"You don't need it, I mean? You've got a lot of laundry."

She smiles, and a few years vanish from her face. "This is nothing," she says. "You oughta catch me after baseball practice."

"Kids?"

"Three boys, two girls." She's happy to talk, Roy can tell. Wants adult conversation. "And the washer in our building is broken, so I have to haul out here between dropping 'em off at school and picking 'em up."

"Hard run, but they're a blessing. Came from a big family, myself. Seven of us. All tight as we can be. Got so where we didn't know when the next meal was coming, but . . ."

"But you gotta have faith," she finishes.

"That's the truth. Now we get together, family reunions—you know, a weekend here, a weekend there—nobody closer than me and my brothers and sisters. Kinda thing that bonds you, you know?"

The woman smiles, and Roy turns to his laundry. Piles the shirts, the pants, the boxers, gets it all ready to go. He doesn't want to put it in the washer yet. Maybe he won't need to. This feels right. She feels right.

"You have kids?" asks the woman. Roy knows he's got her now.

"No," he replies. "We—we tried, but—we thought about adopting. . . ."

The woman nods knowingly. Stops talking. Puts out a hand, pats him on the arm. She's worried she's put him in a bad state. Doesn't want to press the matter. Roy grins meekly and goes back to the laundry. As he reaches down to pull out another shirt from the pile, his right hand digs quickly into his pocket. Snapping motion, barely seen. The lottery ticket flutters to the floor. The woman doesn't notice. Yet.

Roy throws his whites into the washer and closes the lid. He's fumbling in his pockets now, fumbling for change. Comes up with a few quarters, but his fingers get caught up in the shirt he's holding; a quarter flips out of his hand and next to the woman's feet, skittering up against the soles of her tan sandals.

"One got away." Roy grins, and the woman smiles back. She reaches down to pick up the quarter, and for a moment, Roy thinks she's missed the ticket. Thinks she's passed it right on by.

But she stops down there, back stooped. Grabs the quarter with her left, the lottery ticket with her right. "I think you dropped this, too," she says, coming upright.

Roy looks at the ticket, really makes sure to soak in a good glance. Shakes his head. "Nope. I don't play the lottery."

"Me neither," she says. "I did, once, but—my husband made me stop."

"Maybe there's a lost and found."

"Maybe . . ." But she doesn't mean it. Doesn't look around.

Roy lets her off. "I doubt it. Places like this, people come, people go, they drop things. What's the date?"

"Looks like the second. Yesterday's drawing."

Roy looks around. The couple in the corner are still making cutesy-face. The black man has left. There's just one other guy near the door, reading a newspaper. Roy waits for the woman to come up with it. Let her own the moment.

Ten seconds later, it's there. "We should see if it hit," she says.

"Hit? Oh, the lottery, if the numbers hit." Roy pretends to think it over. As if he's got better things to do with his time. "Sure, that'd be fun. We could split fifty-fifty. Three or four numbers come up, we could take home a couple of hundred bucks."

The woman is game. They shake on it. She eagerly leaves her washing machine in search of a newspaper, fingers still clutched tight around that ticket. Roy's glad she took the ticket with her. It always works better when they take the ticket with them. Like it's their property. Found money, but *their* money. He watches as she approaches the man in the corner with yesterday's newspaper and asks to borrow it for a moment. Frankie gladly obliges, and can't help but shoot a wink at Roy when the woman turns around and walks back to the washers.

"What section is it in?" she asks.

"Dunno," says Roy, starting to lay it in. "This isn't my town, so . . ."

But she's found it quickly enough. Section B, page 2, yesterday's winning lotto picks. The woman slaps the ticket across the paper and begins to match up the numbers. It doesn't take long.

"Holy Jesus," says Roy. "Holy Jesus . . . Five outta six. Christ, we were this close, ya know? Some days . . ."

The woman opens her mouth, closes it. Barely speaking, voice almost too low to hear. "That's—they match. These five, they—they match—"

Roy purses his lips. "Too bad. Well, it was good to meet you—"

The woman grabs him by the arm. Pressing down hard. "Five out of six counts. It's not as big, but . . ."

The woman runs a finger along the newspaper. The payouts are printed below the winning numbers. Five out of six, clear as day, a ninety-eight-thousand-dollar win. As the woman starts to check the numbers again and again, Roy sets it all off. "No, no, no," he mumbles under his breath. "No, Jesus, no, no . . ." He whacks his forehead with the flat of his palm, smacking himself good. Does it again, the skin flushing, turning red. "Jesus, no—"

"Wait, wait," protests the woman. "You don't understand, we won. We won. Look at that, it's a hundred-thousand-dollar jackpot, look at that!"

"Dammit, no—"

"Stop, sir, stop—the paper, the paper says we won." She's lowering her voice now, looking around. Fingers practically ripping the ticket in two. It's her ticket, her hundred grand. No one better take it. "You don't understand—"

"No," says Roy firmly, keeping his voice just as low, "*you* don't understand. I—I'm not . . . I'm not supposed to be here."

"The Laundromat?"

"This city. This state. I—ah, Jesus, this is the luck I get. I'm supposed to be in Kansas City. I'm supposed to be at a roofing convention, and I'm . . . My *wife* thinks I'm at a roofing convention."

"Your wife."

"In Kansas City. But I'm not, I'm . . . Hell, I'm involved with a woman here. Downtown. And if I—"

"I see," she says.

"If I come home with fifty grand, that's great, you know? But it ain't exactly the thing you can pretend you won gambling with the boys after hours." Roy rubs his eyes, slaps his head again. "All the dumb luck, huh? All the dumb luck."

She stares at him mutely. Roy doesn't want to lay the last part in if he doesn't have to. He prefers it when *they* come up with the plan. Then it's their idea. Their ticket. Their cash. Everything is theirs, and nothing is his. That's the way he likes it.

"Jesus, lady, I need the money, but I don't wanna get divorced." Then, to finish it, "You take it. You got five kids, you need that kinda cash."

But she won't hear of it. "We said we'd split it. At least, we'll figure something out. I could send you half after I cashed it in, after I got the check—"

"And it's still money comin' in she doesn't know where I got it. My wife ain't the shrinking-violet type—she sees the bankbooks, you know? No, I'd have to come home with poker money or some horse race money or something like that. Too much, and she'd be on me like . . . well, she'd be on me."

Roy lets it sink in. Gives it time. Watched pot doesn't boil, same goes for the mark. He needs to let it take hold. He rubs his eyes again, looks up at the ceiling. The tiles are filthy, encrusted with grime. He looks away.

"I may have one idea," says the woman, dropping her eyes. Roy takes her hand in his, cupping it tight.

"Anything," he says softly. "Let me hear your plan."

||||||||

SHE COMES out of the bank holding a small black bag that Roy has given her. He told her it was for toiletries, for the trip he'd taken out here. She'd watched as he pulled out the toothbrush and the combs and the mouthwash, and she'd taken it inside the bank.

Now she's holding it out in front of her, clutching it to her chest like a newborn. Eyes darting to either side as she walks through the parking lot, hands tight around the handles. Roy waits by her station wagon, leaning against the rusted trunk. Roy doesn't think they make this model anymore.

"I feel horrible," she says as she approaches. "This isn't enough."

"It's more than enough," Roy explains. "Any more, and I'm in deep. This was a wonderful idea, a perfect idea, I can't thank you enough."

"I just—I just wish there was more," she says. "It's all there was in my account. I thought it was closer to seven thousand, but we used some to get the car fixed up last month, so it's closer to six."

"It's perfect," he says. "My wife—she won't know, I can tell her it was from poker, and . . . Heck, I'm done with all this fooling around, anyway, I broke it off last night, but—God, I feel like a heel—"

"No," says the woman, "no, you're not. We all—everyone has their mistakes."

"Mistakes, yeah . . ."

"I wish there was more I could give you. Maybe I could send you some more money later on."

Roy shakes his head and opens the car door for the woman. She gets in, Roy helping her into the seat. "Bless your heart," he says, "but this is best for all. You go cash that ticket in, buy some toys for those rugrats of yours."

She looks up at Roy. Into the sun. Eyes squinting, trying to block out the glare. "Can I at least give you a ride to—"

"No," he says. "I'm going to grab a cab. Give me time to think about this. What I did. You go on now. Go home."

The woman closes the door and guns the engine. Smoke

pours from the exhaust. The car is badly in need of more repairs. Roy steps back, waves, watches as she pulls out of the parking lot and down the street.

A tingle in his throat. Roy thinks about his pills. Watches the birds.

Frankie's car pulls in two minutes later, music pumping, windows pulsing with the beat. He's happy, Roy thinks. Because of the money, because now he can spend a little more. He opens the door for Roy, and the sound pours into the parking lot, trumpets flattening the air. "Turn it down," Roy yells.

"What?"

"Turn it down before I get in that damned thing."

Frankie kicks the stereo down a notch and Roy throws the bag onto his partner's lap. Frankie opens it up, and there it is, in crisp hundred-dollar bills. "Bank fresh," he says, rifling the edges of the money. "I love it. How much?"

"Somewhere between six and seven. She wasn't specific." Roy takes his seat and closes the door, clasps on his seat belt. "Call it six five for good measure."

"Greedy little bitch," Frankie says, gunning the engine. The car squeals out of the parking lot and onto the street. His smile is gone, his good mood turned sour. Six thousand isn't good enough for Frankie. Roy has a feeling that on a day like today, twenty-six thousand wouldn't have been good enough, either.

"That's all she had," Roy says. "That was her savings account."

"Bullshit!"

"Bullshit to your bullshit, that was all the money the broad had, trust me. I can read it."

"Yeah, but six grand's no payoff for a hundred thou, right? She got out easy."

"There is no hundred thousand."

"That's like . . . six grand to a hundred grand, that's some lousy fucking ratio. Can't do the math, but that's a lousy fucking ratio for you and me."

"Frankie," says Roy, slowing down his words, *"there is no hundred grand."*

"Sure, but *she* don't know that. Greedy little bitch."

Roy reaches for the can of warm soda in the drink holder. The aluminum is hot to his touch, the liquid inside probably stale and flat. But he drinks and he drinks, and he washes the bile out of his mouth. He washes the bile that's trickling up, crawling up his throat. He might vomit, right here, right in Frankie's filthy car, but he's hoping he won't. He takes another sip, then goes for Frankie's drink, finishes it off. The stinging fades. The bile is holding off. He's washing it all down. It's okay now. It's okay. It's all going to wash away.

EIGHT

DR. KLEIN doesn't make him wait this time. He's shown into the doctor's office as soon as he arrives, and walks down the wood-paneled hallway without being told where to go. It's been a week of the new medicine, and he's been feeling better on it. Not better as in cured, but better as in not as bad. Better as in it takes twenty minutes to leave the house instead of sixty. That's all he's looking for right now.

"Any side effects?" asks the doctor.

Roy shrugs. "Mouth's been a little dry."

"That's common. You may want to drink more fruit juice, it might cut that down a little."

Roy nods. He doesn't drink much but soda right now. "But it's been pretty good. Different from when I had the pills from Doc Mancuso. I don't feel so . . . slow. You know? I mean, don't get me wrong, the Anafranil was good stuff, but—"

"But sometimes it dulled the edges. Right?"

"Right."

"It's an older class of SSCI compounds, the Anafranil," says

Klein. "The one I've got you on has a stronger inhibitor, but doesn't get in the way. . . ." He trails off. Leans back, glasses perched on the edge of his nose. "But that's not why you're here, to talk about chemistry."

"Hope not." Roy laughs.

"So let's talk."

"Talk . . ." Roy says, trying out the word. "What about?"

"About anything. Whatever you like. Is there anything that's been weighing on you?"

"Like how?"

Klein puts down Roy's file and crosses his hands. "Something you want to get off your chest, something you'd like to tell somebody, anybody. That's what I'm here for. Tell me stories."

For a moment, Roy wants to tell him about the woman at the laundromat. He wants to tell Klein what he does for a living, how he makes his money. He wants to lay it all on the line, get it all out and start over. He wants to describe the laundromat woman. Examine her in every detail. The crappy rings, the crappy car, the crappy life. The bleached hair, the bad skin, the look in her eyes. The six thousand dollars he took from her, every cent of it. Three grand of it sitting in his house, topping off his ceramic statue. Half a drop in his bucket. He wants to tell him about the grift, about every game he knows and every game he wants to know. He wants to tell Klein everything he knows about everything he does.

"Nothing I can think of," Roy says. The carpet, he notices, is still very dark.

Klein pauses. Waits. Roy shrugs. "Well, let's see . . ." the doctor finally says. "Last time, we were talking a little about your ex-wife."

"We were?"

"I was, mostly. You weren't that interested, if I recall, but I thought today, since you're feeling . . . a little better . . . I thought perhaps we could explore it a little."

"I dunno," Roy says. "I was hoping we could just shoot the shit, you know? Sports, whatever, and then you'd give me another bottle."

"We could do that. We could. Same thing, though. Couple guys, sitting around, hey, how 'bout them Mets, them Dodgers, them Cubs, how's your life, how's things, how's that ex-wife of yours . . ."

Roy can't help but grin; Klein has an easy way about him. He almost likes the guy. "You wanna know about Heather?" Roy says.

"If you're ready to talk about it."

"Sure I can talk about it, but it ain't that interesting."

"Boring stories are my specialty," says Klein.

"Okay," Roy says. "I'll tell you about Heather."

SHE WAS nineteen when they met, nineteen and well aware of her body. She moved like a belly dancer when she walked, and like a gymnast when she made love. There was nothing inflexible about Heather. She was open for anything, for fun and excitement and danger. She wasn't there when you needed her and usually there if you didn't. Heather was always on the fringe, always looking in. Never getting caught.

Roy caught her. He was eight months out of a failed army stint, discharge papers in his back pocket. Angry at nobody and everybody all at the same time. He fought a lot those days.

Drank a lot, too. Forgot most of the fights. The club that night was known for its brawls. Roy had never been. He would never go back, either.

She was dancing in the middle of a crowd of men, her long, waist-length hair shaking to the music. Ass wrapped up tight in leather pants. Halter top cupping the small, firm breasts. Center of attention on the lower left quad of the dance floor, and she knew it. Flaunted it. Later, once they were dating, Roy found out that she'd rub her nipples before stepping out onto any dance floor. She wanted them out like that. Needed them to announce her presence. That was Heather.

Roy was out that night with a buddy, a kid from the old neighborhood. He'd just been dumped, needed a trip out. But the guy was morose. Cried in his beer and wanted to leave. But Roy saw Heather at the bar and ordered her a drink. They had a cocktail together, they talked, they laughed. He put his hand on her ass, and she didn't move it. After a bit, another man, a man she knew, came to the bar and dragged her onto the dance floor. Roy didn't mind. Roy could wait.

He sat at the bar for an hour. Waiting patiently for the crowd to disperse, for the songs to end. For Heather to leave the circle of men, to come back to the bar. But the next song came on, and the dancing went on. More men joined the group. Heather and five guys. Surrounding her. Pressing against her. Groping her. Roy began to feel that pressure under his head, the one that made his neck hot and his vision blurry. It was the same feeling he got right before . . . right before he got his discharge papers.

He hit the dance floor. Tapped one of the men on the shoulder. "Cut in?" he shouted over the music. The guy didn't even turn around. "Cut in?" Roy yelled again. This time, a hand appeared in front of his face, palm pressing into his nose. Pushing away, pushing at him.

The feeling grew stronger, that terrible pressure under his hairline, like something was trying to get out. Something roaring inside. He tried again, tried to muscle into the circle, but the writhing bodies bounced him out. In the middle, he could see the girl dancing. Her hair, her breasts, her laughing lips.

When he tried to cut in again, one of the men—a boy, really, a skinny redhead no older than Roy—stepped out and pushed him hard across the chest. "Why don't you leave it alone?" he yelled. "She's ours now."

Roy still doesn't remember exactly what happened, but every time he tells the story, he can recall a little bit more. Like a collage, adding parts each time.

He caught that boy's wrist, snapped it back, bent it, broke it in two. Bone poking through skin. Screams pierced the nightclub air, fighting with the music. The pressure increasing, his head expanding. An arm, caught up in his, a shoulder beneath his palms. Roy, dropping to one knee, exerting pressure, pulling back, and a pop. A squishy pop. And another man down and screaming. In the military, Roy had excelled in his hand-to-hand training sessions.

Two minutes later, and the circle was clear. Heather and Roy stood on the dance floor, Roy's vision clearing, the club coming back into view. Five men on the ground, howling in pain.

Heather didn't know what hit her, but she was in love.

They moved in together two weeks later, and got married a month after that. Five-minute ceremony by a notary who worked at a shipping shop. Roy didn't have a job, and when he found one, he usually lost it quick. Heather didn't care. She loved the sex and she loved having her own place to come home to. They lived in a rented room inside a broken-down farmhouse, but it was theirs. She could scream if she wanted. She could wear what she wanted. Roy loved her for all of it. She was still nineteen.

Twenty when she got pregnant. Didn't tell Roy for two months, but by then it had all gone away. Heather didn't come home some nights, and Roy would spend the evenings in his car, driving the streets. Finding girls who looked like Heather. Beating up their boyfriends. Vision blurred. Finding bars nearby. Going through the motions. Roy hit Heather when she told him about the pregnancy. Hit her when she said she'd been hiding it. He'd never beaten a woman before, never would again. He hit her on the shoulders, on the legs, in the face. Stayed away from her stomach, even with his vision blurred and the pressure straining his head. She had bruises for weeks, she moaned for weeks, and then she was gone.

She was four months pregnant when she left. She was just beginning to show, a small belly on that supple body. Roy didn't try to find her. He knew there was no point. She didn't leave because of the beatings. She didn't leave because of the baby. She left because she was Heather and he was Roy, and they never should have been Heather and Roy. The papers came in the mail a month later, and Roy signed them without reading. Like his signature could erase the memory. He stayed in the house for three straight weeks, and when he came out, the air was clear. It had rained, and it was over.

||||||||

"AND DO you think about her?" Klein asks when Roy's done with his story.

"Not really," he says.

"What could have been, what might have been?"

"What's the point? I got things to do in my life, I can't be thinking about ancient history all the time."

The doctor scratches his chin. "And the baby?"

"*If* there's a baby . . ."

"If there's a baby," Klein echoes. "Do you think about that?"

Roy is silent for a moment. "I have. Sometimes. Just 'cause—it's not for Heather, you know, it's . . . You put something out there, part of yourself. So is there a Roy Junior running around? He look like me? That sorta thing."

Klein nods. "He'd be, what . . . fifteen?"

"Fourteen, fifteen, yeah."

"Ready to become a man."

"I guess." The chair cushions have become uncomfortable. Roy squirms. "There a point to all this?"

"We're just talking, remember? No points unless you say there's a point."

"No," says Roy after a time. "Unless . . ."

"Yes?"

"I dunno. Sometimes I think it might be good to know if there is a kid. Not to see 'em or anything or interfere, but just so I *know*. That make sense?"

"Certainly. Certainly. You know, Roy, there's nothing wrong with a man calling his ex-wife to say hello. Even with the . . . problems you two had. It's done all the time."

Roy can't think of it. He tries to picture himself calling Heather, picking up the phone. But the bile wells in his throat.

Climbing up, burning. He shakes his head. "Nah, I'd—better off the way it is. Don't need that. Got no use with a kid."

"Not everybody has to have a use," says Klein.

"You're a good guy, doc."

Dr. Klein stands and walks behind his desk, opens a file cabinet. "We'll talk about it more next time, if you like," he says, and pulls out a bottle of Roy's pills. Tosses it across the room. Roy snatches it from the air, pockets the bottle. "This is a month's supply, but I'd still like you to come back every week. Will you do that?"

"Just to shoot the shit?"

"Like today."

"Sure," says Roy. "Sure, I'll come back."

||||||||

THREE WEEKS later, and Roy is watching Frankie set up a blow-off on a Spanish Prisoner game they're working three towns over. The stiff is some Joe from a dry-cleaning convention and he's about to put down three big in the hopes that his money will allow Frankie's younger sister over in Romania to bring the family fortune back to America. It's a gag with gray hairs, but it still runs nice at the conventions.

Roy's not involved in this one; he helped to steer the guy in, but he's been staying out of it ever since. Time to rest. The last few weeks have been productive, maybe the most productive in the last year. Nothing big, nothing too long-con, just short games run at breakneck speed. He's got energy these days, and he can feel it. Yesterday, he pulled on an old pair of pants, and they almost fit. Waistband didn't compress his stomach.

And Frankie's been on the ball, filling in where he used to

slack off. Sharpened up his cue under Roy's instruction. Good to see. Good partner, that Frankie. Getting better every day.

When it's all done, when the mark's been blown off and Frankie's back in the car with the three grand, he and Roy whoop it up. Get drive-through burgers 'cause the diner is too far away. Roy takes a pill with his meal, burger in one hand, drink in the other, knees on the steering wheel.

"You still taking them things?" Frankie asks.

"Every day."

Frankie nods, sips his drink. "That's good, that's good. Told you that doc was a good guy."

"Good judgment."

"You say that *now* . . ."

"What?" asks Roy. "What's that supposed to mean?"

"It means I can give you fucking medical advice but I can't steer a hot item our way, that's what it means."

"I don't know what you're talking about."

"Saif," Frankie yelps. "I'm talking about Saif."

"The Arab."

"The Turk. Or Afghan, whatever—yeah, him. I been trying to set up a meeting for months. I'm telling you he's a good guy, he's ready to do business, and every time I bring it up, all you do is crap over it."

"I do not."

"You do, you take a massive dump over the whole thing."

Roy maintains, "I don't see where we need it."

"I need it. Trust me on that one, okay? I need it. I got guys."

"Yeah, I heard about your guys."

Frankie finishes off his burger. He's not letting up this time.

"I'm telling you, there's some real money in this thing, and all I'm asking for is a meeting. One little meeting, and that's it."

Roy doesn't understand why Frankie's so agitated, but it doesn't matter. He's got his quirks, his little tweaks, but he's been a good partner for years. He's more on top of things than he ever was before. These fights, they don't help anyone. Throw him a bone. "One meeting," Roy says. "You set it up, time, place. And if I don't like the guy—"

"We split. No problem."

"I'm saying even if I don't like his goddamned *hair*—"

"Then we're out," Frankie says quickly. He's excited. Like a kid, Roy thinks. A kid with his first after-school job. "It's all your call, Roy."

"Bet your ass it is."

"You won't be sorry. We're gonna be swimming in cash, I promise you."

HE'S BARELY inside the door when the phone starts to ring. He locks the door, fights the urge to unlock and lock it again, and heads into the kitchen. The carpet is looking good. Helps not to look down. Helps to *imagine* it looking good, and take it from there.

"Speak," Roy says into the phone.

"Roy?"

"Yeah?" Suspicious. It's not a voice he knows.

"It's Dr. Klein."

Roy relaxes. "Hey, doc. We gotta reschedule?"

"No, no, not at all." The doctor sounds excited. Excited and nervous. Roy pulls out a chair from the breakfast bar and sits down. "I've got some news."

"About Heather?"

"Yes and no. Yes."

Over the last few sessions, Roy had opened up. About Heather, about their relationship. The few good times, the many bad. And Dr. Klein had gotten him wondering. Mostly about her, but a little about the kid. About the possibility of a kid. And though Roy wanted to know, he couldn't bring himself to call. To talk to her. Every time he thought about it, played out the conversation in his mind, the bile rose up, choked him off. Once, he had to run to the doctor's bathroom, kneel by the toilet. Dry heaves. Spittle drenching the floor.

But the doctor said he'd do it. It was unorthodox, it was unusual, but he would do it. Call Heather on Roy's behalf. See if she wanted to talk. If so, it would be a step. Maybe then Roy could put words together. Couldn't hurt to try.

"I found her," says Klein. "I found her across the state."

"Where?" asks Roy, and then a second later, "Wait—don't tell me. Go on."

"I found her, and I called her, and we had a . . . a nice conversation."

Roy swallows. No bile yet. "Does she want to talk to me?"

A deep breath from the other side. A sigh. "No," Klein says eventually. "She doesn't."

"I see."

"She didn't understand that it might help you with your therapy."

"You told her I was in therapy?"

"I told her I was a psychiatrist, yes. I can't lie, Roy."

He slumps lower in the chair. "So she doesn't want to see me."

"No. No. But there's good news, Roy. Very good news."

Roy laughs bitterly. "She's got cancer?"

The doctor is silent for a moment. The phone line hums. "Was that . . . a wish, Roy?" he says quietly. "That's a lot of rage we should work out—"

"It's a fucking joke, doc. Wake up. C'mon, what's the other news?"

He waits a second, just to build it up. Roy holds his breath. "You have a child."

Exhale. Roy knew it was coming, felt it as soon as he picked up the phone. This was why Klein called him at home. Heather could have waited until the next session. But a kid . . . "What's his name?" asks Roy.

"Angela."

"He's a—it's a girl?"

"Funny name for a boy, huh? Yes, Roy. You have a fourteen-year-old daughter named Angela."

"Jesus. Angela, huh? Nice name, I guess."

"And she wants to meet you."

Roy takes a deep breath. Holds it. This wasn't something he expected. The doctor was supposed to talk to Heather. *Talk* to her. Meetings weren't until the future, that's what they had agreed upon. But a kid. A daughter.

"When?" he asks.

"Whenever we can arrange a time and place. She's got school, but there are weekends, there are evenings."

"Can you do it?" says Roy.

"I can, but you should really be the—"

"Do it," Roy says. "You set it up, and I'll see her."

||||||||

THERE'S A park two miles away from Roy's house. It's got swings, it's got benches, it's got a castle up on a hill. A nice park, a good place to meet. This is where Dr. Klein decided to have the meeting. This is where he's going to bring Angela.

She's coming in by train, Roy knows, but he didn't want to pick her up. That was an option the doc gave him. Pick up your long-lost daughter at the train station. Something about it didn't work for Roy. Made him feel odd. Lots of people at a train station, no room to move. To maneuver. He prefers this meeting in the park. It's open. There are bushes here, places to go if he gets sick.

Roy arrives early. He didn't tell Frankie about the meeting. It didn't seem right, but he didn't tell him. Maybe once it's over, Roy figures. Maybe then, when he's already met his daughter—Angela—when he's already met Angela, then he can tell his partner about her. That he's got a kid. Until then, Frankie thinks he's at a regular appointment with the shrink. That kind of thing he understands. Frankie's mom was a good lady, a real nice lady who made them eat until they burst and never said a bad word about anybody. Then, five years ago, she started seeing things, screaming at the walls. Yelling at Roy when he'd come over, cursing at him. Calling him names. Talking filthy. So Frankie understands about shrinks. About pills. He just might not understand Roy having a daughter, that's all. It can wait.

He takes a seat on a bench, wiping off the bird shit with a

handkerchief. Roy put on one of his best suits for this day, black with a yellow tie. The shirt is loose on him, bunching up at the waist where more of his stomach used to be. The collar is loose, too. Usually it pinches his neck, cuts off his air. Today, there's an inch of space up there. Roy needs some new shirts, he knows, but he likes the feel of these big ones. Likes to feel the space.

Families running through the park. Kids running from their dads, laughing, screaming. Roy wonders if he missed that. Doesn't feel like he did, but he knows he should. Maybe once she gets here, Angela will want to be chased around. What if she asks him to carry her piggyback? Roy doesn't know what he'll do.

As he waits, Roy takes stock of the other people in the park. A few singles, like him, walking along by themselves, jogging, bird-watching. For each one, he instantly comes up with the perfect con. Can't help himself. The lady over by the duck pond would be an easy touch for the covered-message scheme. Young man under the tree, a perfect setup for the Spanish Prisoner. Run the twenties on any of 'em. Roy thinks Klein would fall for nearly any con he ran. Shrinks play analytical, but they're the easiest touch of all. Roy wonders what Angela's hook will be. Is she the kind of girl who'd fall for long-con? Is she the kind of girl who'll take off on short? Would she rat? Would she fold? Until he knows these things about her, he won't understand her. After he knows these things about her, there's no need to understand her. He feels good today.

A sedan pulls into the parking area fifty feet away, and Roy knows without looking that it's Klein's car. It's the kind of thing he would drive, the kind of thing a man in his situation wants to drive. Not too flashy, but comfortable. Proper.

Dr. Klein steps out of his car, sees Roy, and waves. Roy waves back. The windows on the car are tinted, but Roy can see a wash of hair inside the passenger seat. Heather's hair. Long, thick. For a moment, Roy thinks Klein's brought his ex-wife along, and suddenly he's off the bench, on his feet, looking for a tree, a bush, as the vomit rises in his throat—

A girl. Not Heather, just a girl. She steps out of the car, long auburn hair pulled into a ponytail. Shorter than Heather, better posture. Delicate features, pert nose, eyebrows arched in confidence. Slim figure, long legs for her height, budding breasts, and Roy thinks how beautiful she'll be when she's all grown-up, that she'll be just the kind of girl that he likes. He stops. Closes his eyes, shuts it out. Daughter. She's his daughter.

When he looks up again, they're closing in. Angela walks next to Klein, not shy, not overly anxious, just walking. She catches Roy's eye and smiles, her lips turning up, dimples poking in. Roy tries to find something of himself in her. The ears, maybe. The lips. He's not sure. He doesn't know his own face that well.

"The traffic," Dr. Klein begins, looking at his watch, "it was . . . there was a mess down at the station."

"No matter," says Roy. "Don't worry about it."

"You haven't been waiting long?"

"No, no, forget about it."

Klein steps back, puts a hand on Angela's shoulder. "We've been having some good discussions on the way over," he says. "Roy, this is Angela."

The girl sticks out her arm, thrusts it right out there, and Roy grabs and shakes. Her hand is small inside his, a plum in his fist, and he wonders if it was even smaller once. What that would have felt like.

"Good to meetcha," says Angela. Her voice is high. Perky. Roy thought it might be this way. Heather spoke this way.

"Yeah, yeah, good here, too. You sound—you sound a little like your ma."

"Yeah?" says Angela. "Everybody says I sound like Lisa McPherson."

"I dunno," Roy says. "Who's that?"

"Girl who went to my school a while back. She does the news now on Channel Nine."

"And you sound like her?"

"Guess so. That's what people say, anyway."

Dr. Klein steps between them. "I've got a three o'clock back at the office—I'm sorry to take off like this—"

"It's fine," Roy says. "We've got it from here."

Klein smiles, pats Roy on the back. Most people don't pat Roy on the back. Not more than once. But Roy doesn't say anything. Klein didn't mean anything by it. "She's got a train back home at eight o'clock. If you need me to—"

"I can get her there," Roy says. "I can take her. If that's okay . . ."

"Sure," Angela squeaks. "That's great."

Dr. Klein shakes Roy's hand, shakes Angela's hand. Waves and walks away. Back to the car, guns it up. Roy watches as the sedan pulls out of the parking lot. Watches it go down the street. Easier to look away than to start the conversation.

"So," Angela says. "You're my dad."

"Guess so," says Roy. "That's what—that's what Doc Klein found out."

"Cool. Thought I didn't have one, you know."

"Your mom didn't tell you about me?"

Angela shakes her head. "She told me you were dead."

Roy swallows. "Oh. I see."

"I mean, I saw pictures and all, but I didn't know. . . . I figured that was that, and so I didn't think about it much." She looks up at Roy, who is having trouble looking back. "Hey, you wanna go on the swings?"

Roy doesn't fit too well in the swing seat, but he grabs tight onto the metal chain and pushes off. Angela's already flying back and forth, legs whipping through the wind. "That doctor guy was nice."

"Doc Klein?" Roy says. "Yeah, he's a good egg."

"We talked on the drive over. After the train."

" 'Bout what?" asks Roy.

" 'Bout stuff. His wife."

"He's got a wife?" Roy asks.

"Uh-huh. You didn't know that?"

Roy shrugs. "We mostly talk about me. When I see him. What's her name?"

"His wife? Lily," says Angela. "He showed me a picture. She's pretty. And we talked about how things are going, what my mom's like, what she says to me, what she does. I asked him some about you, that sorta thing."

"What'd he tell you about me?"

Angela swings higher, legs kicking longer. "That you were all by yourself, that you were anxious to see me. Not to scare you off, that sorta thing."

"Scare me off?"

"I dunno. I said he was nice, not smart." She slows down again, coming even with Roy's lethargic swinging. "You got fatter," she says plainly.

"Yeah?"

"Yeah. From those pictures I saw, at least."

Roy shrugs. "People get older. They get bigger."

"Some guys get skinnier when they get old. All skin and bones, all wrinkly. Little old guys on the street, they weigh like twenty pounds."

"Little old guys, huh?"

"It's okay, though—you being fat and all," she says, coming to a halt. Her feet drag in the dirt. "I think you look nice. And it looks like a healthy fat, you know. Like you played football or something and now you just don't play anymore. You're not rolling around or wheezing or anything."

"So your mom had pictures of me around?"

"Sorta. Found 'em under a bunch of old junk in the closet when I was looking for some shoes. After that, she had to tell me who you were."

"In the closet . . ."

"At least she didn't cut your face out," says Angela. "My friend Margaret, her mom got a divorce, and she cut out every picture of her dad. Just the face, though, so like, when you're looking at the picture, there's Margaret, and there's her mom, and there's some guy standing next to them only it's empty where his face is supposed to be. It's weird, it's like Freddy Krueger got to 'em."

"Freddy who?"

Angela laughs and jumps off the swing. Her ponytail bounces past Roy's nose, hair tickling his forehead. She bends down, legs apart, hands on her knees, staring Roy in the eyes. Her irises are bright blue, sparkling, like Roy saw in the mirror this morning. Maybe that's what she got from him. Maybe she got his eyes.

"You got a car?" she asks.

"Yeah, I got a car."

"Then let's go for a ride."

THE WAITRESS at the diner isn't surprised to see Roy, but she didn't expect him without Frankie. Certainly didn't expect him with a girl, not a little girl like that. She thinks about calling the cops. Decides against it. Maybe he's got a niece or something. Maybe he's doing the kid a favor.

"Tables open, Sandi?" asks Roy, and the waitress spreads her arms wide.

"Place is yours. Take your pick."

They find a booth off to one corner and sit. Roy doesn't want to be too close to any other patrons. Maybe someone's seen him in here, running a game. He and Frankie don't usually play the short in their own hangouts, but sometimes, when they're bored . . . Like those college kids and the card trick. Doesn't want a scene.

"What's good here?" Angela asks.

"Everything. I guess everything. Mostly, I have the turkey."

"On rye?"

"On rye, yeah."

Angela beams. "That's how I like it."

"No shit?" says Roy, quickly clamping his lips. "No kidding."

She laughs, a high, lovely sound. A giggle, still, but almost a laugh. Right on the edge. "I'm fourteen," she tells him. "I've heard the word *shit* before."

"Better not to use it."

"Sure, but sometimes it's all that works. Shit happens, shit hit the fan—sometimes you've got no choice."

Roy opens his menu, stares down at the words he's seen over a thousand lunches. "Still, better to—there's no need for it, that's all I'm saying." He doesn't want to lecture the girl. Doesn't want to give her rules. Just met her, after all. His fault for using the word in the first place. "Forget it," he says.

Angela shrugs. "Whatever." She looks down at the menu, runs her finger along the edge. Roy can't help but watch as she pores over the choices. Sticks her tongue out of the side of her mouth while she thinks. Heather used to do that. Roy smiles.

The girl looks up, catches him. Smiles back. "Know whatcha want?" she asks.

"Turkey on rye."

"Me too."

Sandi takes their orders, brings them drinks. Sodas on both sides. They sit silently. Roy looks away most of the time, but glances back and forth at his daughter. Trying to find more features, more similarities. Her shoulders, maybe. The chin, perhaps.

"So, what do you . . . for fun, what do you do?"

"Hang out, mostly," she says. "With friends. Movies, run to the mall. Play video games."

Roy nods, as if he does the same things. "That's fun."

"Yeah, it's okay."

Silence again. Roy clears his throat, begins to speak, but Angela cuts him off. "Look, we can just sit quiet until the weird part passes, if that's okay with you."

Roy is grateful. He chuckles a bit and nods his head. Angela sits back in the booth and looks around the diner. She takes the clips out of her hair and rearranges her ponytail, fixes her bangs.

The food comes quickly. Roy picks at his food, tearing at the turkey with small bites. Angela packs it in.

"You're gonna get a bellyache like that," Roy warns.

"Nah. I ate a whole pizza once from Pizza Hut, and I'm not talking about one of those personal pan pizzas. I'm talking about a large pizza, like eight slices, and it was deep dish. I can eat anything—well, almost anything. Mom ever make you that chicken and mushroom sauce thing?"

"Don't remember."

"You'd remember if she had. Now *that'd* give you a bellyache."

Roy grins. Thinks back. "Your mom and I, we didn't eat in a lot. Mostly dinner out, mostly fast food or places like this. Or clubs. Olives on the go."

"I can't get into clubs. There's one club, it's for under eighteen, but it's a drag. Wednesday nights it's twenty-one and older, but they card. There was this guy at school who could drop your picture into PhotoShop and screw with it so you'd get a kicking fake ID, but Robyn Markson got caught and now she can't drive until she's like thirty or something."

Roy doesn't even know where to begin. "Wednesday night's a school night."

Angela rolls her eyes. "I didn't say I go there, I just said they card."

"Oh."

"Mom doesn't care about school nights."

"She doesn't, huh? You're in . . . what?"

"Ninth."

"You do good?"

"I do okay. I do good in Computers. And Social Studies."

"Yeah? What's that, like geography?"

"And history and government. All that stuff. Mrs. Capistrano, the teacher, she's cool, she lets me hang out in her room during other classes." Angela's food is all gone; she starts in on the garnishes.

"Ain't they important, too? The other classes?"

"Sure, but—"

"Listen up," says Roy. "Real important. You gotta go to all the classes."

Angela leans into the booth. A smirk on her face. Roy knows that smirk. That's his smirk. "School's real important, huh? You like it?"

"I didn't."

"Didn't what? Didn't like school?"

"Didn't go. Past the second grade, I didn't go."

Angela sits back. "Hm. That why you ended up a criminal?"

Roy blinks his eyes. Why did she say that? Why would she use that word? "Your mom been telling you stories?"

Angela starts in on the lettuce again. Between bites, she says, "She didn't come right out and say it or nothing, but I kind of got the idea."

"Wrong idea."

"So what kind are you?" she asks, ignoring him. "You don't look like a bank robber—"

"You done with that food?"

"—or a murderer. Definitely not a murderer. I'd see that, you know? My class took a trip once down to the county prison. They said it was so we could see justice in action, but I know they just wanted to scare us outta our heads. Anyway, while we were down there, this one prisoner was being taken back to his cell, and he was all chained up, and the guards walked him past us, and I stopped and looked in his eyes. He looked back at me, too—he did, right at me—and I knew that he'd killed someone. Didn't know who, but it was someone. That's what murderer's eyes look like. You don't have murderer's eyes."

Roy can't believe where this conversation has ended up. "Are you finished?"

"I still haven't guessed what kind of criminal you are."

"I'm not a—"

"It's okay, you know. Everyone's done something bad in their lives. Everyone. If you make it a career, it's just a lot of somethings strung together."

"I'm not a criminal," Roy insists. "I'm an antiques dealer."

"No, you're not."

"Yes, I am. I deal in antiques. I buy them and sell them, period."

"Oh," says Angela. Her tone lowers a notch. "But when you were with my mom, were you—"

"I was a stupid kid when I was with your mom. I did a lot of stupid things, and I regret them all. That's it. It was fifteen years ago, I made mistakes."

"Sure." She's far away now. Looking over his shoulder. Down at her hands. "It's ancient history."

Roy eats again. Angela is quiet. Roy wonders if he's said the wrong thing, if he's screwed something up. He hopes not. This was good, this meal. Sitting down for lunch, forgetting about the con. Just talking. Like with Dr. Klein, only it was closer. Like talking to himself. Over lunch. Pleasant, in an odd way.

"You got a Dairy Queen nearby?" Angela asks, her blue eyes shining in the fluorescent diner light. Roy nods, and his daughter smiles and claps her hands. He hopes that all is forgiven.

|||||||||

ROY OPENS Angela's door outside the train station and helps her out of the car. A steady stream of passengers pour in and out of the revolving doors.

"You got everything?" he asks. "Your purse, your book bag—"

"I got it."

Roy reaches into his pocket and pulls out his money clip. Slides a hundred-dollar bill off the top, hands it to the girl. Her eyes widen. "That's for something to eat on the train."

"Jesus." She laughs. "What, they're serving caviar?"

Roy laughs, too. "No, I just thought—you need cash, right? For a drink or something."

"Hundred bucks for a Coke? You don't get out much." Roy grins, and Angela nods toward the station. "You wanna come inside? I got like a half hour to wait around. I was gonna do some studying, but if you wanna come talk, we can—"

"No," says Roy. "No, you go inside. Do your work."

"You sure?"

"Yeah, I gotta—" In an hour, he's got to meet Frankie down at the docks. But he's not going to tell Angela that. Strange thing is, he wants to. "I gotta meet a client for dinner."

"An antiques client."

"Yeah, an antiques client."

"Uh-huh." She folds the hundred-dollar bill into her pocket, other hand on her hip. Grabs her book bag by the strap and hauls it up and onto a delicate shoulder. From inside, she withdraws a pen and a pad of paper with cats on it. Scribbles something down.

"This is my cell phone," she says, handing the sheet of paper to Roy. "Mom got it for me last year when I had a phone-a-thon with Becky. We were on the phone for sixteen hours straight, no breaks. Becky's mom took away her phone privileges for a month, but I got my own mobile. Pretty cool, huh?"

"Pretty cool."

"Anyway," she says, "you call that, and you get me. You don't have to worry about talking to my mom."

"I don't worry about it. In fact, you tell her I said hi, okay?"

"Won't do much good."

"I know, just tell her I said—"

"I'll tell her, I'll tell her."

Roy sticks out his hand, and Angela pumps it. His arm is pulled close, and he follows the motion as Angela leans up, on her toes, stretching. She kisses his cheek. It's small. Soft.

"See you next week?" she says.

"Next week?" He can still feel her lips on his cheek. It's wet there. Cool in the breeze. "Sure. Sure. Next week."

Roy watches as his daughter hikes the bag up on her shoulder and walks away, into the train station. A few young men standing on the steps watch her go, too. They watch too much. They leer. Roy's first instinct is to smash their heads in. To break their arms so they can't touch her. To crush their legs so they can't follow her. To choke off their windpipes so they can't talk to her.

But there's no pressure there. No pain in his skull. No bile rising in his throat. Everything's working out fine. Angela disappears into the crowd, her ponytail swishing behind her, blending in. She's gone. Roy can't remember what he was angry about. People walk past him on all sides, moving to and from their destinations. The revolving door spins around again. Angela's still not there. He climbs back into his car and drives away. He's got deals to make.

SEVEN

FRANKIE'S CAR is already parked at the docks when Roy pulls up. His headlights are cut, and the music, for once, is off. Roy is glad. He likes crooners as much as the next guy, just not that loud. Not that often. Roy pulls into a space, his tires banging over the warped wood beneath. Hard to see out here. He turns off his engine and waits outside the car. The breeze is warm. He can hear the water nearby, the sounds of the ocean. Smell the dead fish. They rot under the docks, that's what people say. They get caught at low tide and wedged against the wood. Caught there until the water recedes, and they die, flopping around. Sun bakes down, sometimes they explode. Fish guts under the docks. That's the smell of the docks. That's the smell of the ocean. Roy doesn't come down here a lot.

He waits by the car because it's too dark to see. Doesn't even know where they're going. It's Frankie's setup, all of it. If it goes down right, if this Turk character is who Frankie says he is, then it will be worth it. Odds are, he'll blow it off as soon as he hears the setup. It doesn't sound right already. Roy doesn't like bringing in partners. He doesn't work with partners, except for those he's known for a long time. Frankie's been with Roy for seven, eight years. Running the C together for at least five. They've got a good thing going. Before Frankie, it was Hank, and before Hank he didn't run the con. It's a lineage, a line of succession. Hank, Roy, Frankie. Clean, no scars. No need to spoil it now. No need to get caught at low tide.

"Roy. Roy." A whisper, insistent, from behind him.

"Frankie?" He can't see past ten feet out here. The lights are few and far between, dim. The moon is behind clouds tonight. "Where are you?"

"Between the buildings. Look down, follow the yellow line."

A thin strip of paint circles the perimeter of the dock, and Roy keeps his eyes down as he goes. Like he's walking a tightrope. Soon, he can see Frankie's slim body in a small alleyway between two warehouses. He's got a duffel bag with him.

"What's in there?" Roy asks.

"Plastic."

"For what?"

"For the art. If we wanna transport it."

"The art."

Frankie starts to walk. Roy's right behind him. "The art, the art from—look, let's just meet with the guy, and you'll see, okay? Okay, Roy?"

"Yeah, okay, that's what I said. Let's meet with him. Go, lead on." Art, he wants to talk about. What does Roy know about art?

"So you check this thing out?"

"It's sweet, you're gonna love it. I tell you, you're gonna be flying."

"But did you check it out?" Roy asks. "Everything?"

"I told you. I known Saif two years."

"From where?"

"I know him, don't worry about it."

"Yeah, and where from?"

Frankie picks up the pace; Roy tries hard to follow. "Where I know him from? My sister's boyfriend's friend, if you gotta know."

"Tight connection."

"Fuck you," Frankie spits.

"All I'm saying is, this thing better be clean—"

"It's clean."

"—'cause the last thing I need is to be staring down a barrel."

"It's clean," Frankie insists, "it's clean. Jesus, you're a hard sonofabitch to work with, you know that?"

Roy grins behind the darkness. They come to a warehouse door, the small entrance next to the fold-up receiving bay. Frankie knocks once, twice. The door opens.

The warehouse is tall. Twenty, thirty feet. Rafters disappearing after the drop ceiling, low-watt lights hanging down. Crates, boxes litter the floor. Foam on the walls, blocking out noise, blocking out light. Tarps just beyond. Insulated. Roy likes the protection, likes the thought that went into it. Smart.

"Frank!" Inside the warehouse, coming toward them. Happy to see them. "It is good to see you. You look well, my friend." An accent, thicker than Roy imagined. Doesn't sound like the other Arabs he's done business with, but there haven't been many.

Frankie grabs the arm of the tall, broad man approaching them. He's dark—dark skin, dark hair. Thin mustache across his upper lip. Sharp nose. Doesn't look like an Arab. Maybe this is what Turks look like. He kisses Frankie on the cheek, hugs him close. Frankie hugs back. Roy puts his hands in his pockets. This must be Saif.

He breaks off the embrace and holds Frankie at arm's distance, pointing at his upper lip. "A little fuzz, yes? Working on that mustache we talked about?"

"We don't do facial hair," Roy cuts in.

Saif cups an ear. "You don't do . . ."

"Facial hair. Identifying mark. They'll pick you outta a lineup first thing with a stash like that."

Saif's laugh booms throughout the warehouse, sinking into the foam walls. "I like this one already," he says to Frankie. He goes to hug Roy, gets a hand instead. They shake.

Roy looks at his watch. He's got nowhere to be, but he doesn't want to spend the rest of the night at the docks. He can smell the fish, even inside. "Let's get cooking on this." He turns to Saif, cutting Frankie out of the conversation. "My friend here tells me you've got some slag you want to run. I'll tell you right now, we don't fence."

"I am aware of this," says Saif. "Frankie tells me this. But this is not your usual . . . slag, as you said. What I am looking for is a partner, one who—"

Frankie cringes even before Roy reacts. "Partner?" Roy says. "I think you got the wrong impression. We don't take partners."

"But surely you must work with others."

"It's a give-take relationship, and I take."

"And Frank?"

"Frankie's been my guy for years. He was gonna screw me over, he'd have done it a long time ago. You, I'm not so sure about."

Roy turns to leave, but Frankie steps forward, working his

way in. Trying to turn Roy around. His tone is clipped, fast, nervous. "Look, maybe we got off on the wrong foot here. Roy, Saif is clean, I'm telling you—"

"You can take my merchandise anywhere," Saif protests, hurt. His volume rises, dark face flushing. "It is the best merchandise. You ask anyone in this town about Saif, they will tell you I am a good man. Ask anyone."

"He's just real cautious," Frankie tells Saif. "He didn't mean anything by it." Spins to Roy, who's already turned his back on the two. "Roy, Roy, it's clean. You said we'd look at it, you said we'd check the deal."

Roy sighs. He's cautious. He's right to be cautious, he knows. That's the only way to play it. But caution shouldn't prevent a deal, so long as the pieces are in the right place. Money is money. "Let's see what you got," he says.

Saif nods his head. "I understand your reservations."

"You do, huh? Good. Then that part of our discussion is over. Let's see the stuff."

Saif leads them across the warehouse. Roy takes in all the boxes, all the crates coming through here. "Merchandise comes off the boats?" he asks.

"Directly into my warehouse," says Saif. "I do the shipping. Home routing. Some makes it to its final destination, some . . . some are damaged along the way."

Frankie laughs. Saif joins in. Roy does not. "So if you've already got a fence set up, what do you need us for?"

"Again, friend, this is not precisely a . . . fencing situation. Here, please. Look at this."

Saif is standing by an open crate, six feet high, the side pried off. He reaches into the darkness and pulls out a painting. Matted, but unframed. Muted, splotchy colors. Paint thrown onto the canvas. Abstract art.

"It's a fucking mess," says Roy.

Saif shakes his head. "It's a Pollock."

"Okay, it's a Pollock."

"Not exactly."

Roy looks to Frankie. Did he come here to play games? "What is it, a Pollock or not a Pollock?"

"Both," says Saif proudly. "Neither."

Roy gets it. Seen this scam before. "So it's a forgery."

"Not quite." Saif is grinning openly now. He enjoys this.

Roy does not. "I'm about two seconds from gone."

"Please," says Saif, holding up a hand. "I will explain." He pulls the painting closer, bringing it underneath a strong light. "Look in the corner. There, the bottom right."

There's a signature scrawled in blue paint. Nothing more than a few squiggly lines, but it clearly does not say Pollock.

"So what is it?" asks Roy.

"There is a man in Amsterdam named Philippe Marat, and he is the finest forger of Jackson Pollock's work in the entire world. Original Pollocks are nearly impossible to purchase, even for the fantastically wealthy, because there are so few of them on the market. That is where Marat steps in."

"So like I thought," Roy says. "It's a forgery."

Saif nods. "But not of a Pollock. This is a forgery of a *Marat*."

Roy catches Frankie's smile and begins to understand why his partner brought him here. "It's a forgery of a forgery."

"Marat's work is so popular now that he, too, commands large commissions, and now he, too, is quite rich, and has the luxury of reducing his output. The market for Marats has tripled in the last year, but there are few Marats to be had. That is where my people come in."

Roy doesn't know what to make of it. The painting doesn't appeal to him, certainly. Makes him think about the carpet back home. But some folks like that. Roy's seen people pay up for morgue photos, for autopsy shots. Roy's seen it all.

"People pay for this?"

"People pay good money, my friend. When I worked through my European dealers, these sold faster than any other merchandise I have ever moved. I have many artists like this, many pictures. For every Pollock there is a Marat and a nameless man in Africa. For every Rothko, there is a Gardiner and his counterpart in Sweden, and so on. The prices here in the States, they are much higher than overseas. My fences from Turkey could easily—"

"We don't fence," Roy says again. "I wouldn't know where to—"

"But we know guys," Frankie cuts in. "We got buddies downtown, Roy. We're just talking about being the middleman here, a go-between. We can't lose."

"We can always lose."

Saif purses his lips, nods his head. "I understand your concern. If you are not interested in the art, there are a great many of my countrymen who have entered the trafficking business. Perhaps—"

"No drugs," says Roy. "That's a rule." He approaches the painting, rubbing his hand along the canvas. The paint is hard, thick. Roy is surprised to find that it has a real texture, a firmness to it. "You've got more of these?"

"Hundreds," says Saif. "And more coming in every week."

Roy takes a step back, examines the painting once more. Still can't see the interest in it, but he understands what makes money move. "I don't know art," he begins, walking around Saif. "I don't even pretend to know where to start. Couldn't tell you who this Pollock or Marat guy is, couldn't tell you if this is a good fake or a crappy one—"

"I tell you, it is the finest—"

"—but I'm willing to take your word for it. Why? Because Frankie here vouches for you. And because I'm no judge of art. Or fake art."

"Then I must thank you."

"But there's one thing I do know, and that's the big C. The con. The racket. Don't know what they call it in your country, but we've been doing it over here longer than your people been herding goats. I know all the angles, and I see them coming before other guys even thought of 'em."

"I have no doubt, my friend."

Roy eyes the Turk. His clothes, his hair. The way he stands out from the background, as if none of the objects in the room dare to get too close. "Tell me, you know what a mush is?"

Saif smiles, spreads his arms. "Educate me."

"A mush is just another word for a big black umbrella. Easiest prop there is, but here's the way it went down: Old days, a grifter would sit in the stands at the racetrack on a rainy afternoon and take side bets."

"Side bets?"

"Illegal wagers. You've got ten-to-one odds on some horse in the fifth down at the windows, but the grifter will give you twenty-to-one on the same horse. Folks wanna up their money, they go to the man in the stands. Anyway, he'd be sitting there in the rain, taking everybody's bets, taking in all their money. Cash up front, always. So by the time the race starts, he's got ten, twenty grand sitting in his pocket and three times that in outstanding wagers, but he doesn't care who the winner is, 'cause he's not gonna be around for the finish.

"The second the bell goes off for the race and those horses bust outta the gates, everybody's watching the action. That's when the grifter takes his mush, raises it over his head, and disappears into the crowd and all those other black umbrellas, taking the money with him. And no one at that track ever sees him again.

"If we get together on this," Roy continues, coming back around to Saif, holding his gaze, holding it tight, "and I see you even *looking* to raise your mush, I'll kill you. Just so we have it straight, I'll kill you."

Saif nods his head. His voice is low. "I would expect no less."

"Good," says Roy, all smiles and cheer. "Let's see the rest of this crap."

||||||||

OVER THE next week, Roy and Frankie move eight of the paintings, with promises to deliver more. Their contact downtown, a fellow Roy's known since he was paired up with Hank, knows a guy who knows a guy who knows a guy. Beyond that, Roy doesn't want to be involved. He and Frankie are splitting about eight grand per piece. Roy's satisfied with the take.

The third night they're running the art, one of the pictures catches Roy's attention. Brighter colors than the rest, interesting shapes. It's abstract, but Roy thinks it might mean something if he looks at it hard enough. "This is a Miró," Saif tells him. "A woman from Brussels copying a man from El Salvador copying the man from Spain. Very famous." As thanks for his services, as a gesture of goodwill, Saif gives the picture to Roy, free of charge. Roy pays him a thousand dollars anyway. He doesn't trust anything that comes free.

When Roy goes home that night, he hangs the painting, unframed, above the ceramic horse in the den. It contrasts wildly with the dull watercolors. Brings out the meager light in the room. That night, he sleeps in the den for the first time since he bought the house. Opens up the fold-out sofa and falls asleep right there, staring at the picture. At the forgery from Brussels.

The next morning, Roy wakes up late. Sun streaming in the window, blue sky lighting the room. Barely any time to shave and shower. No time for food. He's got an appointment with Dr. Klein.

"Am I late?" he asks the secretary as he walks in the front door. "I'm late, right?"

Wanda is used to Roy by now. She smiles and waves as he rushes by. "He's running late himself. Go in, don't worry about it."

Klein sits behind his desk, as usual, scribbling on a notepad. As usual. Roy notices a stack of textbooks perched on the desk corner. A duffel bag flung onto the carpet. "Hey, doc," he says, "how's the brain game?" Roy plops down in the chair and makes himself comfortable.

The doctor looks up from his work. "Roy. You're . . . up."

"Almost wasn't. Overslept."

"I mean emotionally. You seem up. Good to see."

Roy shrugs. "Magic pills, doc. Got somethin' special in 'em."

Klein laughs. "They've got an SSCI inhibitor in them, if you want to be specific, but sure—magic pills. It's about time they kicked in like this." He fidgets with the notepad for a moment. Plays with his pencil holder. "I hear you had a nice time with Angela last week. I hear it went well."

"Yeah. It went okay. I mean, I know fourteen-year-olds like I know gardening, right? But we had some nice conversations, I think. It went—it went okay." Roy stops, wonders how the doc knew they hit it off. "You talk to her?"

"I did. I did, and that's something I wanted to discuss with you."

"Something about Angela?"

Behind him, Roy can hear the waiting room door opening. Footsteps padding down the paneled hallway. Light, carefree. He knows she's coming even before he turns around, before he sees her there, plaid skirt and blue blouse, ripping away at a plastic candy bar wrapper with her teeth.

"The machine was outta Snickers," says Angela, "so I had to get a Twix. I hate these things." She looks up, into the room, and sees Roy. A smile leaps onto her face. "Hey, Roy. Nice tie."

She hops into the room and plants a kiss on Roy's cheek. He's not sure if he should give her a kiss back, but by then she's already halfway across the office and sitting in her own cushioned chair. Legs folded beneath her. Bouncing. Like Heather used to do.

"It's—it's Wednesday," Roy says, surprised. "I thought you'd call about—I figured on the weekend—"

"Yeah, the thing about that, goes like this. Basically, I told mom you said hi. Remember at the train station, you told me to tell her you said hi, and I said it wouldn't do any good, and—"

"I remember."

"Right. So I told her you said hi, and she said she didn't want to hear about it. And I told her I thought that it wasn't so bad that you were saying hi, and that if you wanted to say hi, she should at least listen to it. It's one word, right? Hi, that's all. But she said she didn't want to hear about it, and she didn't want me speaking for you. And I said that I didn't think she should decide who I speak for and who I don't speak for, and she said that if I kept telling her you said hi, I'd be grounded. So I told her you said hi, just to see what she'd do, and she actually grounded me. So then I started saying it over and over again, and then she went ballistic, and then I went a little ballistic, and . . ." She smiles and picks up a duffel bag next to her chair, hauls it onto her lap.

"You've got room at your place, right?"

"THIS HAPPEN a lot?" Roy asks her that evening. He's preparing the sofa bed, pulling on new sheets. The den is dark, the Miró covered in shadows. "You leave home a lot?"

"You're not freaked out or anything, right?" says Angela. "It happens sometimes."

"Freaked out? No, I just didn't expect—"

"I stay with friends, usually, girls from school. Doesn't last more than a few days for mom to come down off the ladder, then she lets me back in the house."

Roy fluffs the pillows as best he can. "She still got a temper, huh?"

"If that's what you call it. Sometimes, she's great, she'll get me ice cream, we'll go out walking, just walking, you know? Walk and talk and whatever and she's a pretty cool mom. Lets my friends hang out late, doesn't bother us. Other times, she'll freak out for no reason, go all mad scientist on me. Pulling at her hair, shrieking, spinning in circles. The dog goes and hides under a table. You never know." Angela sits on the sofa bed; it creaks beneath her meager weight. "She like that when you two were together?"

Roy sits on the other side of the bed. It sags. "A little," he says. "Mostly, we yelled at each other, I don't know what started it. I do remember one time when we'd gone out for a bite to eat, late at night after all the clubs had closed. We found this place, a nice place, really, that was open till three."

"Like a diner?"

"Not a diner. Usually it was a diner, but this was a few steps up. This wasn't an after-bars place, this was an after-theater place. You know, folks go to the late show, they wander in for dinner, that sort of thing. Only we weren't part of that set. But we sit down, we order dinner, and we're looking around us at the suits and the dresses and laughing with each other, and then—then I think it was the busboy spilled a little water near her feet. Near your mom's shoes. And I don't know if they were special shoes or not special shoes or what, but she flew off the handle. Flew off the handle, broke it in two, and shoved it up that busboy's ass, is more like it. By the time they threw us out, your mom had broken three place settings and insulted just about everybody in the place." Roy realizes he's smiling as he's telling this story. Good to be talking about it.

"Sounds like mom."

Roy shrugs. "I guess."

"You think she'd still be that way if you two were together?"

He looks at Angela. Innocent eyes. "What's that mean?"

"It means what it means. Maybe mom's angry 'cause she had to raise me on her own."

"Wait a second," says Roy, flustered. "Wait—I didn't leave your mother. I didn't—I didn't even know you—that you were—"

Angela puts her hand on Roy's forearm. Soothing. "That's not what I meant. I'm not blaming you—I don't blame anyone. Mom, maybe. I just thought maybe if you two were still together, it would be easier on her. Less stress."

"Maybe. But I doubt it. I don't—let's not worry about it. It's late, you're tired. I got some business to attend to." He stands, and the bed rises. "If you get hungry, I got deli meats in the fridge."

"I'm okay," says Angela, "but thanks."

"I got bread in the freezer, you just gotta warm it up in the microwave. Mustard in the fridge. There's a frozen soup in there, too, but it's kinda old, so . . . Forget about the soup, there's canned soup in the pantry."

"Really, Roy, I'm not hungry."

"Okay. If you want a drink—do you drink?"

"I'm fourteen."

"Right. Right." He's not sure what she means by that. "So if you want a drink, the liquor cabinet is in the living room, next to the stereo."

Angela crawls into bed, pulling the covers beneath her chin. She moves like Heather, Roy thinks. Like she's swimming through the air. "I gotta go out for a bit," says Roy. "You'll be okay."

"I'll be sleeping. Where you going?"

"Meet a client."

"Another one? At midnight?"

Roy nods, pulls a quilt over Angela's covered body. "Antiques wait for no man."

She giggles and turns on her side, grasping a pillow in her arms. "Night, Roy."

"Good night, Angela."

AT THE diner, Frankie can't stop talking about the art deal. He has plans, big plans, he tells Roy. Ideas and methods and new ways to get the merchandise moving across the country. He has local, regional, global networks. He can see this becoming their main business, their main source of income. All the while, Roy wonders if Angela is doing okay at home. He's wondering if she is sleeping all right. He's wondering if she's woken up and seen the ceramic horse. He's wondering if she's been able to pull off the head. He's wondering if she's looked inside. If she has, he'll have to tell her what he does for a living. If she has, he'll have to come clean.

"And what I'm thinking," Frankie is saying, "is that we take the money that we get from, say, the British sales, and we funnel it back over to the connections we make in Asia. That way, we're dealing with two different sets of funds, two different operations."

"Uh-huh," mutters Roy. His turkey is dry tonight. The mustard isn't helping.

"And then there's currency exchange. If we time it right, we can add on an extra grand or so per piece, just by changing over the money at the right time. I saw this whole financial thing on CNN."

"Right, sure."

Frankie puts down his burger. Stares at his vacant partner. "Thought maybe I'd go home early tonight and screw a hamster," he says calmly.

"Good idea," Roy murmurs. "Sounds good."

Now Frankie's up, halfway out of his seat, throwing his fork to the ground. Roy flinches, awake. "I thought the goddamned pills were working," Frankie growls.

"What? They are."

"Fuck that, then you're not taking 'em."

"I am, I am, what the hell are you talking about? Sit down." Roy looks around the diner; they're causing a scene. Other patrons are looking, talking. Whispering. "C'mon, siddown."

"What the fuck is up with you?" Frankie asks, still half standing at the counter. "Tell me what the fuck is your problem."

"You wanna calm down first, then we'll talk."

"We been talking. At least, I been talking. You've been uh-huh-ing me and mm-hmm-ing me for thirty goddamned minutes. I'm talking about money here, about ways to make us money, and you're off in dreamland."

"That's not it. That's—"

Frankie cuts in. "I know this art money is a joke to you. I know ten grand is a joke—"

"Never," says Roy. "Ten grand is ten grand."

"—'cause you got so much frigging money, comin' out your ears, you and your investments and your . . . whatever you do with it."

Roy doesn't know what Frankie knows. Or what Frankie thinks he knows. He's sure Frankie doesn't know about the horse. And he's sure Frankie doesn't know about the Caymans, the accounts.

Beyond that, he doesn't want to take any chances. Frankie is his partner, and Frankie is a good guy. But Roy's money is Roy's money. No one else need concern himself with it.

"Calm down," Roy suggests. "Just calm down. I don't know where you get the idea I got so much money."

"Come off it. We make the same score, I know what you take in."

"So you got just as much."

"But I spend it. I buy myself nice things. You got a crappy little car and a crappy little house, and suits ten years old. And you're always talking about saving your money, rainy day, anything can happen in the life of a matchstick man, all that crap."

Roy sits back. He breathes deep. Relatively easy. "Where's all this coming from?"

Frankie plops back down onto the stool. The other diners give up and turn away from the show. "The thing is," he says, "I still gotta hustle for my money, you know? I still gotta do the things we do just to keep afloat. And it ain't good for my morale when my partner drops his ass on everything I say."

"I wasn't dropping my ass," Roy says. But he knows he was. He doesn't always pay attention to Frankie. Certainly wasn't tonight. "I was just . . ." Can't find the right words. Frankie's hurt, he can see that. Wants to know things will be right again. Roy can fix it. Roy can explain. Hell. It's gotta come out sometime.

"I got a kid," Roy says plainly. "I got a daughter and her name is Angela, she's fourteen, and she's staying at my place tonight."

Frankie takes a bite of his burger, laughs through the bun. "Bad joke, Roy."

"If it's a joke, I'm still waiting for the punch line." And he tells Frankie the whole story.

||||||||

ALL THE way down to the docks that night, Frankie lets Roy know exactly how he feels about the situation. "It ain't good. It ain't good at all."

"It's temporary," Roy explains. "She had a fight with her ma, she's staying for a day or two until things cool off."

"All I'm saying is, you don't know what having a kid is like."

"And you do?"

"I don't. But I wouldn't take one on just like that—just 'cause my shrink said it'd be good for me."

"She's my—she's from me. I made her. In part, I—look, I got a responsibility now. Some kind of responsibility, whatever. And if that's what it takes to do my part, then that's what it takes."

"It's dangerous."

"It's not." They arrive at the docks, and Roy parks in the same spot, edged up against Saif's warehouse. "She doesn't know what I do, she's not involved."

"Sounds like she wants to be."

"But she's not, and it'll stay that way. You don't wanna see her, you don't got to see her. Period."

Frankie slams the passenger door as he climbs out of the car. Roy lets it go. They stomp into the warehouse, Frankie in front. Roy's got the shopping bags, the money. He doesn't like carrying the money. Makes him nervous. He tries to watch the shadows as he walks, but the footing is tough out here. The rotting fish smell is still around. Roy can't wait for winter.

Saif is there to greet them, as always, arms wide, ready for an embrace. Roy gives in. He let Saif hug him the last time they came, and now he's set a precedent. Price of doing business with Syrians. Or Turks. Whatever he is.

"Forty grand," Frankie tells Saif, taking the money out of Roy's shopping bag, piling it atop a crate. "This is off the Kandinsky and the—what's the one with the black rectangle in the middle and the orange one off to the side?"

"The Wilder," says Saif.

"Yeah, that one. Twenty-five for the Kandinsky, fifteen for the Wilder."

Saif snaps his fingers, and a thin man dressed in a blue jumpsuit comes over, takes the cash. "And your cut?"

"Taken out already," says Roy. "Saves us time. If that's all, we'll see you tomorrow for another pickup." He starts for the warehouse door.

"My friends," calls Saif. "Please, if you have a moment?"

Roy doesn't. He wants to get home. To get to bed. To see if Angela is asleep, dreaming. Safe. He looks to Frankie, whose eyes, hangdog, say it all. Stay. Listen to the man. "Yes?" Roy sighs, turning around.

"Given that we have done so well these last few weeks, perhaps we are in a position to take our relationship further."

Roy shakes his head. "I don't kiss till the fifth date."

Saif grins. "I grow tired of dealing with the same art. I have been doing it for many years, and while it is lucrative, it can be . . . boring."

"Take up a hobby," Roy suggests. "Macramé. Golf. This concerns me how?"

"The hobby I am looking into is your lifestyle."

"Our *lifestyle*?"

"The con. The grift. I am interested in joining your situation."

"I thought I made this clear," Roy says. "We don't take on partners."

"Perhaps as a student—"

"And we don't take on projects."

Saif looks to Frankie. Roy can see they've discussed this before. Frankie nods his support to Saif, and the Turk continues. "I understand that for the larger schemes, the . . . the long-con . . . you need capital."

"We don't play long." They do, but not often. No use telling him that.

"I understand that it can be most profitable. And I have the capital required."

"Money we got. Thanks, but no thanks."

Saif keeps talking, his words flowing over Roy's. "Also, I have many friends with similar funding, similar capital. Many who are looking for a good score."

Roy makes his motions deliberate. Careful steps. Hard steps. He wants it to sink into Saif's thick head this time. "I don't know how many times I gotta tell you this," he says, keeping his tone level. "Maybe I gotta scratch it into your forehead. Maybe I gotta carve it on your tombstone. But since we're doing this art deal together, I'll be nice one more time, and tell you plain: We. Don't. Take. Partners."

Saif backs off. Lowers his eyes. "I see. Perhaps another time, my friends."

Another time. Roy can feel the pressure starting to build in his head, hear the sound of rushing water. The warehouse walls start to blur, and Roy knows he needs to relax. Think about his pills at home. Think about how well they're working. Think about Angela, sleeping in the den. He can't explode right here, right now.

Teeth grinding, jaw clenching, Roy grabs Frankie by the upper arm and wordlessly leads him out of the warehouse, into the fish-air and the night.

Frankie's upset. "That's the kinda thing I'm talking about," he whines. "That's the thing you do—that man wanted to *deal*—"

Roy spins on his partner, faces him down with the first real anger Frankie's seen in years. Now there's no need to keep his tone down. Now there's no need to keep his words deliberate. "Don't you ever go behind my back like that again, you understand me? We got a thing here—this is not how we work. If it's you and me, then it's you and me, and this other fuck don't enter into it, no matter if he's got the cash, you got that?"

"Jesus, Roy, I didn't mean to—I thought you might like the idea."

"What you did—what you wanted to do—that's not business sense, that's a death wish, you know that? How many three-man, four-man games you know of stuck around long enough to watch themselves on the other side of the jailhouse fence? You got another guy, then it's worrying about the other guy. You don't know him long—you know him two years, you say—he could spin around and stab you in the back—fuck that, stab *me* in the back—anytime he sees fit. Take our money and run."

Frankie's cowed, petulant. "You're overreacting," he says softly.

"I am underreacting. I should be throwing you to the fucking seals, that's what I should be doing. Hank always told me when your partner gets itchy feet, don't put the cream on for him. Let him go. You wanna go, is that it? You wanna team up with Saif from now on?"

"No—Jesus, Roy, no—"

"No, you don't." And now Roy's out of steam. The pressure is gone. Released. He can see again, see through the darkness to the car. "Because we make a good pair," he continues, volume lowered. "You and me, we make a good pair. Let's not screw that up. Yes?"

"Okay. Okay."

"Okay. Conversation over."

||||||||

ROY DOESN'T want to wake Angela, but he doesn't want to keep the eight grand in his pocket anywhere other than inside the horse. He knows it's silly. Knows there's no safety in the horse, no more so than a drawer or a cabinet. But it's his way, and pills or no pills, he wants the cash inside that horse.

He tiptoes into the den, holding his breath. Walking on the balls of his feet. It's hard. It hurts his calves. Angela is asleep on the fold-out, covers kicked off her body, arms still wrapped around that pillow. Her nightgown rides high above her knee, and Roy tries to keep his gaze away from her legs. Like Heather's legs. Long. Better to look away. Look at the horse.

The head is heavy, it's always heavy. Tonight, it's made out of lead. The quieter he tries to be, the more noise he seems to make. The ceramic neck scrapes against the body as he lifts. He stops, holds it in place. Beads of sweat break out along the back of his neck. Angela takes a breath, a sleeping snort, and turns over, away from him. Facing the wall. Perfect.

Roy lifts again, and the head pops off. He tries to hold it with one hand, balancing the head against his hip, as he takes the money out of his jacket pocket. Pushes down the pile, squashing the money already inside. Full. Too full. He needs to get to the Caymans, and soon. Too much money in the house. Too much for anyone.

It's easier to put the head back on. No creaks. No scraping. He stands there for a moment, looking at the Miró on the wall. It's like Angela, he thinks. It has life. It's the only thing on these walls with any life. Maybe tomorrow, he'll ask Saif for another one.

"Roy?" Angela, behind him. Roy's heart kicks up a notch.

"Go to sleep," he says, turning around. She's up on one elbow, peering through the darkness. Didn't see him with the horse. Probably didn't see him with the horse. "You just wake up?" he asks.

"Uh-huh. Can I have a drink of water?"

"Sure. Sure. You sit tight." Roy walks into the kitchen, finds a clean glass, and pours her a bit from the tap. Puts in a few ice cubes to make it cold. Dash of lemon to help with the taste. Tap water isn't so good around these parts.

He returns to the den, sits on the corner of the fold-out, and hands her the glass. "Thanks," she says, taking a sip. "It's dry in here."

"It's always dry. It's the winds."

She takes another sip. "How was your meeting?"

"Good. I've got some buyers."

"For what?"

"For a piece I'm selling. A table set. Very old."

Angela smiles, pulls her hair on top of her head. The strands hang down in front of her eyes. All he can see are her lips, and they're grinning. "Can I ask you another question?"

"Tomorrow. Go to sleep."

"Why'd mom leave you?"

This kid and her questions. "You'd—you'd have to ask her."

Angela hands Roy the water glass, lies back down in the bed. Roy pulls the covers over her body. "That was part of the whole mess," she says. "I asked, but she didn't want to talk about it. Called you a few names."

"I'm sure she did. Well . . ." Roy doesn't want to tell Angela about that one time, when his fists got the better of him. Heather would have left him anyway. Eventually. Maybe she saw it coming long before he did. "I don't really know why your mom left me. Maybe she thought I was a bad guy."

"Are you?" asks Angela. Words slurring, arms grabbing for the pillow again. Hugging it close. Dropping back to sleep. "Are you a bad guy?"

"Yes."

"You don't look like a bad guy."

"That's part of it. That's what makes me good at it."

Angela's eyes close, her head sinks lower into the pillow. "I don't think you're a bad guy. I don't think you're bad at all."

"You're young," says Roy. He stands, smooths out her covers, and walks to the door. "Go to sleep." Steps into the hallway, closes the door behind him, watching the light sliver and fade inside the den. Time for Roy to go to sleep, too. He heads for the bedroom.

Five feet away, he can still hear Angela's murmur: "I don't think you're bad at all."

SIX

ROY HAS never been inside this store before. It's a boutique. Low lighting, strange music. One of those places they talk about on television. He has always bought his suits in department stores. Once, he bought a suit at one of those bulk-order discount places, one of those warehouse stores. It still fits him fine. But this place is inside the mall, and this is a place with a famous name. Roy didn't know it was a famous name, but Angela recognized it right off the bat. She squealed and grabbed his hand and led him inside and introduced him to a man wearing satin. Suddenly, Roy was trying on jackets and pants and ties.

"I really don't need this," he says to her. He's got on a blue suit, light pinstripes. Red tie.

"You do. Trust me, you do."

"I don't see what was wrong with my old suits."

"They were old suits."

"They were fine," says Roy.

"I've seen them. And I've got a reputation to maintain. You should, too."

Roy looks at himself in the mirror. The jacket hangs nicely across his chest, hiding the paunch of his stomach. Sleeves don't ride up on his arms. Pants sit on his hips, not squeezing at his waist. It's not such a horrible thing to have something that fits. Something that looks proper.

They find two more suits he likes, two sport coats, some shirts and ties. Angela shuttles back and forth between the dressing room and the racks, throwing things over the top for Roy to try on. She hangs it back up when he doesn't like it, bundles it up to the register when he does.

When they're all done, Angela escorts Roy up to the front. "This is what we call a cash register," she says playfully. "Did they have those last time you bought suits?"

Roy smiles at the clerk. "My daughter. At least until the orphanage takes her back." Angela punches Roy in the gut, and he laughs.

The clerk doesn't care. He rings up the clothes and announces the total. "Six thousand, four hundred eighteen and sixty-five cents. Check or charge?"

"Cash," says Roy.

The clerk isn't sure if he's supposed to laugh. He's not. Roy dipped into the horse before coming to the mall. He's got bigger bills, but the pile of hundreds still makes a show on the narrow counter. Roy counts it out and waits for his change. Angela watches the clerk try to stuff the wad of cash into the register; it doesn't quite fit.

"He's an antiques dealer," she tells the young man. "Business is good."

After three more stores, Angela convinces Roy to get his hair cut. The stylist's name is Daphne, and she and Angela keep up a furious chatter about movie stars all through the session. Roy is relieved. He didn't want to talk.

The joys of the food court are relatively new to Roy. He'd always seen people eating there, but never tried it for himself. He and Angela both choose Chinese, both choose the lo mein. It's her favorite dish, she says. It's his, too. Something else she got from him. The eyes, the turkey on rye, and the Chinese dish of choice. It's a start.

"You got me beat," says Roy. "I never knew shopping was such a workout."

" 'Cause you never went shopping with me. If you want, after lunch, there's a Prada store up in the nicer section."

"Uncle. Lemme digest first, then we'll talk about it."

Angela picks at her lo mein, twirling the noodles around her chopsticks. "Back there, in the store . . . that was real cash, wasn't it?"

"Yep."

"That's a lotta money to just have . . . you know, around. Checks work okay, you know. Lotta people use 'em."

"I don't trust banks."

"In general?"

"In general. I don't trust 'em."

"I don't understand," she says. "You think they'll steal your money or something? Banks are gonna fold on you?"

Roy takes a bite of his food, slurps the noodles into his mouth. "They take your money and they put it out on the street. Car loans, mortgages, whatever. And they give you two percent off their ten percent. They're stealing eight percent from you."

"I don't know anything about that stuff," Angela admits. "I got a C in Math last quarter. All I know is that's a lotta money to have around the house."

Roy shrugs. The small hairs on the back of his neck rub against his shirt collar. "I think she cut it too short."

"She cut it fine. It looks nice."

Roy runs his fingers through the top. There's barely any hair there to muss. "It's like a crew cut."

"It's not. It's nice, trust me. You look nice."

They eat their lo mein. They sip their soda. They watch the people walk by with their trays. Shoppers. Happy consumers.

"If you're a drug runner," Angela says, "you can tell me."

The noodles catch in Roy's throat. He coughs once, twice. Spits into a napkin, swallows what's left. "Excuse me?"

" 'Cause it's all right with me. Everyone's gotta make a living."

"What makes you—I'm not a drug runner."

"It's not like you find a lotta antique dealers running around with huge wads of cash in their pockets."

"It's a cash business."

"So long as you don't sell to kids. That's not cool. You don't sell to kids, do you?"

"For chrissakes," Roy says, trying to keep his voice down, "I'm not a drug runner."

"Then what are you?" The question is simple, precise. She's not kidding this time. Angela leans in.

"I'm—look, what difference does it make?"

"None. I just want to know. What do you *do,* Roy?"

He looks around the food court. Housewives, eating their calzones. Businessmen, getting in a quick gyro and fries. No one seems to be paying attention to them. No one cares.

"I tell you," Roy says, "and then we drop it and finish lunch?"

"Deal."

"I'm talking we drop it, drop it. End of conversation."

"Yes. Deal."

"I'm a con man."

Angela's eyes open wide as she sits back in her molded plastic chair. "Cool," she says, drawing it out.

"It's not cool."

"You're a grifter."

"Yes."

"A bunco artist."

"Yes."

"A flimflam man. Playing the C. Stroking the mark. Taking the chump."

"You know the lingo," says Roy.

"I go to the movies. Oh, man, this is so cool."

"What I do is not a movie. It's not funny, it's not a game. It's—it's what I do, and most of it is wrong. Now I told you what I did for a living, you live up to the deal and finish your food."

"Teach me something."

"Drop it, Angela."

"C'mon, teach me."

"You're out of your—I'm not teaching you anything." Roy doesn't want to eat his Chinese food anymore. He wants to feel the bile rising in his throat. Wants to be angry with her. She shouldn't be asking these questions. Shouldn't be wanting to learn the con. But there's no bile. There's no pressure.

"One trick," she begs. "One, so I can use it at school."

"Jesus. No."

"Okay, I won't use it at school. I won't use it at all. I swear, I just want to know. I want to know how you do it, it's so cool—"

"Listen," he says, pulling her out of the seat, pulling her close. His hand is tight around her, gripping the soft flesh. He can feel her small biceps flex under his fingers. "What I do is not cool. It's not fun. It's taking money away from people who are too stupid not to have it taken from them. And you're too good—you're a good girl, a good person—and I'm not going to teach you something like that."

He releases her. She stands there. Pouting. Not going back to her seat, not eating her food. Pouting.

"Go," he says. "Sit down, eat." But she doesn't budge. Arms down by her sides, shoulders slumped. Staring through him, past him.

"Fine," says Roy, returning to his lo mein. "Stand there. Make that face. I'm hungry."

It's not until they're in the car, four blocks past the mall, that Roy realizes he's getting the silent treatment. It's been years. Fifteen, at least. He can hardly remember what the silent treatment sounds like. Angela sits in the passenger seat, arms folded across her chest, staring at the road ahead. Not pouting anymore, just staring.

"Where you wanna go next?" There's no answer. That's enough answer for him. "You wanna listen to the radio?"

She doesn't even move. Roy is impressed. He leans over and flicks on the radio. Spins the dial. Finds a classical station. He doesn't like classical music, but he's sure Angela likes it less. He turns up the volume. Violins fill the air.

"If you want me to turn it down," he yells over the music, "just say so."

Nothing. Roy tries again. "You want the windows down? I can put the windows down." When there's no response, he hits the electric window switch, and the car is filled with a rush of air, whipping through Angela's hair. Blowing it into her face, across her eyes. Still no movement. The kid is good. Her mother would have cracked by now. Screamed or yelled or laughed, any of the three good enough for Roy. Not Angela. He's proud, in a way.

Roy takes her to a movie. A comedy. People in the theater are laughing. They're laughing so hard they're gasping for air. Nothing but a straight face outta the girl. Roy throws popcorn at her; a piece sticks in her hair. She reaches up and brushes it away. Folds her arms again. Pouts.

And it goes through dinner. Pasta, taken out from an Italian deli near Roy's place. Roy turns off the TV halfway through the meal to see if she'll talk. She doesn't. He turns it back on again. Needs some noise, something happening. Anything. That night, when he puts her to bed, she doesn't ask him questions. She doesn't pester him. She doesn't kiss his forehead. She doesn't do any of the things Angela used to do. She doesn't tell him good night.

Roy goes to sleep, telling himself she'll crack by morning. She's stubborn, she's good at being stubborn, but she's a little girl. She's got to talk eventually. She's got to break down sooner or later.

Breakfast is a silent affair. Like eating in a vacuum. Roy tries, tries hard. "Okay," he says finally, pushing away his cereal. Angela sits opposite him at the table, still in her nightgown. "Okay, two can play at this game."

And that's when Roy starts his own silent treatment. He's quiet. She's quiet. They stare at each other over uneaten bowls of cereal. Eyes locked. Battle of wills.

THE KID behind the counter at the convenience store has just been dumped by the only girl who's ever let him get to second base. Jessica. His Jessica. She had glasses and spit a little when she kissed and was in the smart classes, but she was his. He's sixteen, skinny, pimply, and hates his job. It's the only job he could get, other than bagging at the local grocery. But when he's working, he doesn't want to see anyone from school, and this store is way outside of his neighborhood. He hates the job, but he likes the money it gives him. He can go out on dates with that money. If he had someone to go out on dates with.

It's nearing noon when the girl enters the store. She skips inside, barely waiting for the door to open before dancing into the aisles. Freshman, it looks like. Maybe a sophomore. Pretty. Reddish-brown hair down to her waist, a lot like Jessica's. Better body than Jessica, though. Thin. Long legs. Beautiful lips.

Angela flits down the aisles, making sure she's noticed. Spins up to the counter, running her fingers over the display racks of chewing gum. "You got a favorite?" she asks the young man.

"Favorite gum?"

"Yeah. I wanna buy some, but I don't know what kind. You have an idea?"

The clerk clears his throat. No one ever asks for his opinion. Pretty girls never ask for his opinion. "I like Dentyne," he says.

"Dentyne! Oh, yeah, I love Dentyne." She giggles. Sounds like she means it. "We're like gum twins," and the clerk nods along. Grins. He doesn't know what she means, but he likes it. "What is that, like forty-five cents?"

He knows the gum costs fifty cents, but wants to seem like he's doing his job. Wants to impress. So he runs the gum past the scanner, and the price pops up on the screen. "Fifty cents," he says, voice cracking in the middle. "Fifty."

Angela digs into her pockets, twisting her torso around as she looks for change. The boy tries not to look at her chest, at the soft breasts gyrating right in front of his face. He looks away, beyond her, to the aisles. Back to her face. Concentrate on her face.

"No change," she says eventually. "All I got is this." She hands him a twenty-dollar bill and smiles abashedly. "I feel stupid giving you a twenty for something that costs fifty cents."

He waves it off. "Don't, we do it all the time. Guys come in here with hundreds, they just want water." Pops open the register, makes change. Gives the girl her $19.50 and tries to touch the skin on her palm when he transfers the money. It's smooth, just as he knew it would be.

"Thanks," she says, pocketing the cash. Rips open the gum and pops a stick in her mouth. She leans against the counter, face a mere two feet away from his. "So you go to school around here?"

The young man swallows, prays that his voice maintains its register, and says, "Sorta. I go to Hamilton."

"Really? Cool. I had some friends who went there, they took me to some games. Hey—that's where I know you from. You're on the football team, right?"

He doesn't want to blush. Really doesn't want to blush. Tries to keep his breath even. "No," he says. Wants to embellish, wants to lie, but he can't. "No."

"Are you sure?"

"Am I—yeah, yeah, I—I mean, I would have tried out for the team, but . . . you know, I've got other commitments."

Angela nods her head knowingly. "Shame," she says, reaching out, touching the boy's arm. Stroking his biceps. "Arms like these . . . Well, their loss, right?"

"Right. Sure." Can't breathe all that well.

The pretty girl who walked into his store shoots him a final smile and waves good-bye. Starts to leave, heading for the double doors. He wants to call out, to get her name, her phone number, but he can't work his vocal cords. But suddenly she stops, spins around, comes back to the counter. He's wondering if she's going to ask him out. If she's going to make the first move.

"I found fifty cents," she says, plopping two quarters on the table.

He doesn't understand for a second. What does fifty cents have to do with a date? It kicks in: the gum. The gum. "Oh," he says. "Great." He slides her change into the cash register.

"Can I get my twenty back?" she asks, blinking those big blue eyes.

He nods and pulls her bill back into the open. Hands it to her, watches her pocket it. Stares down at the floor. Easier to talk if he's not looking at her. "Listen," he says, words sticking in his throat, "maybe sometime . . . we could go out or something?"

There's no answer. He's scared to look up. What if she's laughing at him?

But there's no laughter, and there won't be an answer. By the time he finally works up the courage to raise his head, the bell on the front door is ringing and the girl is gone.

Once outside, Angela slows down her pace. Roy, stepping out from an alley behind the store, catches up with her. "You got the twenty back?"

"Yep."

"And the nineteen-fifty he gave you in change?"

"You got it." She laughs.

"That's the twenties," says Roy. "Oldest game on the books. Well, maybe not the oldest, but—"

"God, that was easy. I didn't know it was that easy."

"That's basic stuff. Foundation. It should be easy. It's not all like that."

"I know, I know. It's just that . . . it felt good. Like I was doing something right for a change."

Roy shrugs. He's glad it went well for her. "It's not right. It's just a way of doing things."

"Whatever," she says. "Let's do it again. There's a 7-Eleven down the block."

"No more. We said one trick."

"C'mon, one measly 7-Eleven won't hurt anyone. How'm I supposed to get better if I don't practice?"

"You're not supposed to get better, and you're not going to practice. You're done." This was what he'd worried about. The lure of easy money. First time he ever pulled a game, it was the twenties, and it was all a spiral since then. Hank taught him the ins and the outs of the system, but it was that first game of the twenties that hooked him, dragged him in.

"You want lunch?" he asks Angela. Hoping she won't throw another tantrum.

"Sure," she says. Disappointed, he can see, but not at silent treatment levels. She's a rational girl. She knows the score.

Buzzing, from Roy's back pocket. Like something nipping his ass. Again. He reaches back, feels the hard square of plastic. The beeper. Must be set on vibrate. He hates that thing.

Roy pulls the pager from his pocket and takes a look at the number. It's unknown to him, but there are four extra digits at the end: 2420. That's Frankie's code.

"Ah, crap."

"What?"

"I gotta make a phone call."

Angela cocks her head, smiling. "Urgent antique sale?"

"Knock it off. I gotta find a pay phone."

Angela holds out her cell, but Roy waves it off. "C'mon," she says, "I've got like twenty million free minutes."

"Pay phone," he insists. "That's how we do things." They pick up the pace, Roy scanning the street for a phone booth. There, across the way, by the deli. "Wait here. I'll be back in a second."

By the time Roy's got himself wedged into the small phone booth, he realizes Angela's crossed the street with him. She waves at him through the glass. Roy calls the number on his pager, waits for Frankie to answer.

"Hello?" A voice, unsure. Not familiar.

"Frankie?"

"No, this is Bob."

"Bob."

"Yeah."

Roy is confused. "Bob, did you call me?"

"No. No, you called me. You called this number."

"Right," says Roy. " 'Cause I got paged. I called the number on my pager—"

As he speaks, Roy can hear more voices in the background.

Now it sounds like Frankie. An upset Frankie. ". . . the fuck off the phone, ya fucking moron. Gimme that, *gimme* . . ." There's a scuffle, a few muted gasps. Then Frankie's on the line, loud and clear. "Roy?"

"Yeah, it's me. What's going on there?"

"I'm at the airport. I page you, go to take a whiz, and I come back and some asshole's answered the phone. Who the fuck answers pay phones at the airport?"

"Bob does. What's the problem?"

"I got something cooking here I need you for. Jamaican switch, full-on, been working it for weeks. Guy's ready to topple, set up like bottles on a fence."

Angela's pressing her face up against the pay-phone glass, mashing her cheeks into monstrous proportions. Roy turns away. "I'm in the middle of something here. Can it wait till tomorrow?"

"No can do. He's a nervous nellie, he won't last."

"And he's got the money?"

"On him, that's what I'm saying."

Angela's back in front of him again, a tube of lipstick in her hand. She starts to draw on the glass, and it takes Roy a second to figure out what she's writing: 7-11, 7-11, 7-11. Turns around again. Tangled in the phone cord now.

"What's the pull?"

" 'Round thirty grand," says Frankie. "I told him we'd meet at the bar in the Delta lounge at three."

Roy looks at his watch—it's nearing two. Figuring for traffic and the stops he'll have to make, he can just make it under the wire. "I can do it."

"You grab the papers and setup dough?"

" 'Course," Roy says. "What in?"

"Pounds."

"Am I supposed to be English or something? I can't do that goddamned accent—last time you pulled that French bullshit—"

"American banker," Frankie says, laughing. "Be as Midwest as you want."

"Okay. Three o'clock, bar in the Delta terminal." Angela has now marked up the other sides of the phone booth with bright red lipstick. The numbers 7 and 11 stare down at him from all angles. She dances and skips around the perimeter, laughing and smiling and waving at Roy inside. He knows he should think about what to do with Angela. He knows there's no time to drop her off. He knows there's no way she'll go for it. "And I'll bring the distraction."

Frankie doesn't understand. "You'll bring the what?"

Roy hangs up. Exits the phone booth. "Who was it?" Angela asks.

"It was business."

"Oooh," Angela squeals. "Can I help?"

Roy picks up the pace, almost into a jog. Angela keeps up. "Yes."

"Really?"

"Really. I'm not happy about it, but I got no choice. You do what I tell you to, and we'll all come out of it fine. You want practice, you're gonna get practice."

"So what's my job?" she asks. "What am I gonna do?"

"You're gonna throw a temper tantrum. Think you can handle that?"

Angela laughs all the way to the car.

FRANKIE AND the mark are already sitting at the short table inside the bar. Roy can see them through the frosted-glass window. A drink in front of each, nervous glances on the mark's face. Eyes shifting around. Roy checks his watch; he's five minutes late. They had to drop by the house, call a friend of a friend down at the bank's exchange parlor. Five minutes isn't so bad.

He's got a briefcase in his right hand, a simple black briefcase with gold snaps. Nothing odd about it. Nothing special. There are thousands like it in the city, in any city. It's the kind of briefcase Roy prefers for these jobs. Hank used Gucci knockoffs for the Jamaican switch, but Roy always thought it was ostentatious. Pointless. Waste a good fake like that.

He checks his hair in the mirror, adjusts his jacket. He's wearing one of the new suits they bought yesterday. The kind of suit a banker would wear. Roy's decided that he's from Rhode Island, if the matter comes up. Doesn't want to play Midwest.

"Good to see you," he says as he enters the bar and sidles up to the table. He shakes Frankie's hand, doesn't want to say his name. Doesn't know what name Frankie gave to this guy; easier not to use anything.

Frankie makes introductions. "Chuck," he says, turning to the mark, "this is Arden Davis, the banker I told you about."

They shake. "Pleased," says Roy. "Chuck, is it?"

"Charles," says the man. "Chuck, if you want. Look, I don't know if I'm comfortable with this."

Roy sits down, smooths out his jacket. He places the briefcase on the floor next to his feet. "You're not comfortable?"

"With this. With this . . . This is all very fast."

"What is it?" Frankie asks. "Is it the airport?"

"It's the airport, it's—"

" 'Cause we can go somewhere else." Frankie turns to Roy. "You've got a flight out, right? Where are you going?"

"Dallas. One of our corporate clients wants to set up a funding account that bridges the franc and the lira, so I've got to go down and explain the ins and outs of the thing." He laughs, pulls a passing waitress to his side. "Hon, can I get a martini? Thanks." Back to the conversation. "This is what I do all day, explain money to people."

Roy's speech hasn't seemed to cool the mark out any. He's still got those shifty eyes Roy doesn't like. "You got concerns," Frankie says. "I got that. Let's talk 'em out."

Chuck shakes his head. Pushes away from the table. "It's not that. It's—there's a lot of money we're talking about here, and—"

"And I'm trying to help you," Frankie says. "Hell, I'm helping myself, too, let's not bullshit here. But this is win-win across the board. If I'm wrong, lemme know."

"No, no," says Chuck, "I agree, but . . ."

Frankie nods to Roy, who reaches down by his feet and picks up the briefcase. He hauls it up and onto the table, where it lands with a dull thud. Roy checks to make sure there aren't any onlookers, and pops the locks. Aims the opening toward Chuck, and slowly lifts the lid.

Pounds. Real British pounds, stacked up in hard bricks of bills. Filling the briefcase from end to end. Chuck swallows hard. "Is that . . . is it all there?"

"Thirty thousand pounds," says Roy, closing the briefcase and locking it back up. He lowers his voice to a whisper. "This is one of the perks from working in the exchange program at the bank."

"Arden is vice president," Frankie explains. "Gets in on the high level. You have your end?"

Chuck pulls his own briefcase onto the table, pats the side. Frankie pulls it close and pops the lid. American bills, stacked in the same method as the pounds. "Thirty thousand," says Chuck. "Like we said. But I don't know if I'm . . . I just don't know . . ."

"Christ, man," says Frankie, sitting back. "We're doing you a favor. You get thirty thousand British—what's that going for, Arden?"

"On today's rate . . ." Roy pretends to think for a second, as if he's doing the math in his head. But he memorized that figure a half hour ago. "Around forty-nine thousand, eight hundred."

"Forty-nine eight," Frankie repeats. "We do the switch, that's almost twenty grand American for you, for sitting on your ass and helping out a friend of mine. You know how many people'd jump at the chance . . ."

Frankie goes on, gently beating Chuck down. As he talks, Angela steps inside the bar. Roy raises his eyebrows. She starts to walk. In her right hand is a briefcase. Black, simple, plain. Gold snaps. Roy drops his hand, and she stops a few tables away.

"I know, I'm being paranoid," says Chuck. "I know. But where's it coming from? Whose money is it, you know?"

Frankie's incredulous. "Whose . . . you gotta be kidding me."

Roy ignores Frankie. This is the part where the roper is supposed to fade out of the picture. He brought the mark in, and now the closer takes over. But Frankie's not good at fading out of anything; Roy always feels like he's wresting control from his partner. Maybe next time they'll switch roles. Doubtful.

"It was extra money," Roy explains. "Unaccounted for. Floating on the top of the books, like a layer of cream."

"And you just . . . scooped it off?" says Chuck. He's coming onto the deal, getting excited.

"Exactly. Exactly."

The waitress makes her way over to the table, martini balanced on her tray. Roy raises his right hand, scratches his nose. With perfect timing, Angela arrives behind their table at the same time as the waitress. As the server bends down to give Roy his drink, Angela uses her body as cover, dropping the briefcase next to Roy's feet.

Once the waitress leaves, Chuck drops his volume. He's wrapped up tight now. "So what you're saying is, this is basically embezzlement, gone through a sifter."

Roy loves it when they bring up the term. People shy away at your average garden-variety mugging, but when it comes to white-collar crime, they're all up for a percentage. "If you want to call it that. Heck, I'd take the money for myself, but I can't do a thing about it, 'cause I'm under tight watch at the bank. I got audits and security crawling around me. They'll know if I change a single peso."

Chuck's got it. "So if we exchange it here, just us . . ."

"Then they don't need to know. You can take these pounds and go change them anywhere you want. Hell, there's an exchange booth right inside the airport here."

"Wouldn't recommend that," says Frankie.

" 'Course not," adds Roy. "But I'm saying, for him, it's safe. No scrutiny."

Chuck thinks it over, but Roy knows he's ready to go. "Okay," he says. "How do we do this?"

"Nothing too hard," says Roy, pointing down at the table.

"We've got two briefcases here. When we stand up, you take mine, I take yours. Then you walk out, we wait here a bit, and I walk out. Done."

"Seems . . . easy," says Chuck.

"It is."

From the far side of the bar, a sudden commotion. Loud conversation, incoherent. Shouting. A high-pitched voice. A young girl. "I don't need no goddamned ID," she's yelling. "This is a fucking *airport* bar, whattaya gotta see my ID for?"

The bartender is trying to talk to her, trying to keep it down, but it's no use. The girl grabs a tumbler and screams, "I'll break every fucking glass in this place. I'll do it, too, don't think I won't."

When the glass starts flying, crashing along the floor, everyone in the bar turns to see the commotion. Chuck included. Frankie, too. Roy takes the opportunity to yank the briefcase with the pounds off the table and exchange it for the one Angela brought in. He slides the first briefcase under his chair, out of sight. The switch takes less than two seconds.

As quickly as the scene began, it comes to an end. Roy watches Angela put on the capper to her show, tears streaming down those cheeks. She storms out of the bar, cursing at the top of her lungs, tossing a final shot glass back over her shoulder for good measure. The bartender catches it before it hits the ground. The crowd applauds.

Things return to normal in the bar. Silence for a moment, filled in by the rush of average conversation. Roy looks at his watch. "We'd better finish this up. Chuck, it's been good doing business with you." They shake hands, and Roy nods down to the briefcase on the table. "Go ahead," he says. "Take it, have fun. Go on vacation. I hear London's lovely this time of year."

Chuck smiles nervously and grabs the black briefcase. "I should . . . go first?"

"Better to give us some time," says Frankie. "So we don't walk out together."

"Of course," says Chuck. He thinks of himself as a master money-launderer now. "Sure, of course."

He grabs the handle of the briefcase and lifts it to his side. The heft is good, weighing down his shoulder. Fingers shaking a little. Arm shaking a little. He sets his sights on the entrance and makes his way out of the bar, knees wobbly.

When he's gone, when a good minute has passed by, Frankie turns to Roy. "How long you figure before he opens the briefcase and finds the newspapers?"

"Parking garage," Roy says. "Inside his car."

"Then we'd better get going."

"Meet you at the diner?"

"At the diner," Frankie says. "And Roy—that . . . distraction. Was that yours?"

Roy nods. He knew Frankie wasn't going to like it. "Yeah, partner, that was mine."

Frankie nods. He looks away from Roy. Won't meet his eyes. "At the diner," he says. "Let's meet at the diner."

FIVE

ANGELA IS still giddy over the afternoon's events. She eats her turkey sandwich, barely able to remain seated. "I threw that one glass," she says, "and it shattered hard. I mean, I didn't think I threw it hard enough to break that much, but did you hear it? It was like an explosion."

"You did real good," says Roy. It's hard for him not to smile. She's excited. She did a good job. But Frankie's not happy. Frankie's not happy with it at all. He came into the diner once they were already sitting down, barely registered Angela's presence. Roy tried to introduce them, tried to get Frankie to acknowledge his daughter, but there wasn't much. A handshake. A grunt. Angela tried, but Frankie just ordered his burger and shut up.

"Almost got cut by some of it," Angela continues. "I jumped back, though. Did you see that old chick by the counter? The one with the makeup? She almost died when I threw that glass."

"You did good," Roy repeats. Turns to Frankie, tries to include him. "Didn't she do good?"

"Yeah," he mutters.

"Hit her cue, right on time."

"Was it okay I yelled so loud?" Angela asks.

Roy nods. " 'Course. Loud's the way to go. I said have a fit, hell, you had a fit."

Angela says, "Frankie?"

"Hm?"

"Was it okay?"

"Yeah. Sure, loud. It was great."

Roy can't have this. Frankie and Angela not talking. Frankie never shuts up, and now, tonight, he's a clam. He can't operate like that, not tonight. Not if she's around. He leans over the table. "Take it easy, okay?"

"Take what easy?" says Frankie. "I'm easy."

"What's your problem?"

Frankie looks away. "No problem."

"Thirty-G take, I hope there ain't a problem."

Frankie starts to talk, then stops himself. Closes his mouth. Looks to the girl, to Roy. Digs in his pocket, comes up with a bunch of quarters. "There's some video games a few stores down," he tells Angela, tossing the quarters onto the table. "Why don't you go play?"

"If you're gonna talk about me—"

"We're not."

"—I'll stay."

"We're not gonna talk about you. I got business to discuss with Roy."

Angela shakes her head. Folds her arms across the table. "So I'll sit here and eat. I won't bother you."

"I ain't saying you're bothering me, I'm just saying . . . Roy?"

He doesn't want to be in this situation. Not a decision he wants to make. "Let the kid stay," he says. "She'll sit there, eat her turkey. Go on, eat your dinner."

Angela smiles and tucks in, pointedly turning her body from the other two. Frankie shakes his head. "This—this is what I've been talking about all along."

"You have a problem me bringing her into this thing. Understood. It was dumb."

Angela cuts in. "But I did real good, you said it."

"Shush. Eat." Roy turns back to Frankie. "It was dumb, but it couldn't be helped. You called me outta the blue, I had her with me, what was I supposed to do?"

"That's the thing, you're the one screaming no partners all the time."

"Different situation," says Roy.

"Same situation. Exact same situation. She's just as much of a liability to us as any other guy we bring in. Saif, Howard from the water plant, whoever." Frankie's not paying attention to Angela now. She's watching them argue, and he doesn't seem to care. "We got just as much exposure 'cause of her as we do with anyone."

"You're wrong," says Roy.

"What if Chuck goes to the cops?"

"He won't."

"What if?"

"They never do. We've run this six, seven times, right? Same thing happened there will go down with Chuck. He'll leave the airport, get into his car, he'll open the briefcase, he'll find ten pounds of old newspapers instead of the money. Twenty seconds later he'll figure out he's been had, but he's not gonna run to the cops, because it was an illegal trade in the first place. That's why the switch works so good."

"But it doesn't *have* to work that way," says Frankie. "He did nothing illegal. No funds were actually traded. He was robbed, plain and simple, and maybe he realizes that. Maybe then he doesn't mind a trip to the local sheriff's office."

"So?"

"So maybe he faces us."

Roy's not swayed. "They're gonna sketch a pair of bunco dealers? For one take? Forget it."

"Right. And we've never been arrested, so our mugs aren't on the books. We're safe."

Roy takes another bite of his sandwich. It's good tonight. "So we're safe, what's the problem?"

"I'll tell you what the problem is. Maybe he remembers a commotion at the bar. Maybe he realizes that's when the bags were switched. Maybe he remembers the face of a little girl. Maybe he adds two and two and gets four."

Now Frankie's got a bead on Angela. Staring her down. She gives it back. Neither one flinching. "And maybe he faces her. And maybe the law's got some picture of that little girl. Maybe she's been in trouble before. So they track down her mother, who tells them where to find her. And then they come knocking on your door. Worse still, then they come knocking on *my* door." Talking to Roy, still staring at Angela. "That's why I got a problem. Partner."

"Glad you shared that," says Roy. He feels like Dr. Klein. Understands now what it is to listen to a rant. "But you don't have to worry about that. If that's your concern, we're in the clear. Angela's never been mixed up with the law." He turns to his daughter, who has scooted a few inches farther down the booth. "Go, on," he says to her. "Tell him and let's get this over with."

Angela smiles at Roy. At her father. Not her usual grin. Forehead tight. Raised. Heather had that look. He doesn't remember what it meant. "Come on," he says, "let's finish this thing so you two can be friends. Tell him you're clean, Angela. Go on, tell him. Angela?"

She takes another bite of her sandwich. Suddenly, Roy is very tired.

"I WOULD have told you," she says on the car ride home, fighting through a veil of tears, "but it didn't come up."

"Come up? Come up? You're *fourteen*—when did you have time to get arrested?"

"I forgot to pay for a pack of cards, that's it. I bet when you were fourteen, you were in trouble."

"You're a girl, for chrissakes. When was it?"

"I dunno, two years ago."

"And they called the cops on you." Roy's feet are leaden. He can barely keep his arms on the steering wheel. "They called the cops 'cause you stole a single pack of cards."

Angela shrugs. "I mighta put up a fuss when the security guy nabbed me."

"Angela . . ."

"Jesus, Roy, he was groping me. He was grabbing at my tits, what was I supposed to do, let the little fuck cop a free feel?" She's shaking now, angry.

"No—no, that's not . . . You just should have told me, that's all. These are the kind of things I need to know."

She curls up on the seat, bringing her knees up to her chin. Sniffling. "It's not the kind of thing I like to talk about, okay? Forget about it."

"What's done is done. But it's Frankie I'm worried about."

"What about him?"

"He doesn't like you."

"Good," she pouts. "I don't like him, either."

Roy shakes his head. Clears it. The road ahead is fogging up. "Can't have that. Can't have that at all. He's my partner."

"I can be your partner."

"*He's* my partner. You're . . . along. And I can't have my partner and my . . . you . . . eyeing each other. Even if you and him never see each other again, I can't have that. Got enough going on in my life without a feud. Just . . . be cool with him, okay?"

Angela comes out of the fetal position. Puts her feet up on the dashboard. Roy doesn't mind. Recognizes the action, but doesn't mind. "If he's cool with me, I'll be cool with him."

"Thank you. Any other arrests I should know about?"

"In this country?" asks Angela, blinking her eyes rapidly, innocently.

"Angela."

"Felony or misdemeanor?"

"You're a funny girl. You know that? You should have a show."

"Arrested or booked? And convicted or acquitted? You've got to be a lot more specific about your questions, Officer." Angela laughs and pounces on Roy, throwing her arms around his big shoulders. He holds tight to the wheel, tries to keep the car straight. She plants a firm kiss on the side of his head and plops back in her seat.

"I've screwed up before," she says, "but I'm a pretty good person, Roy. That's what my mom says. So till you teach me otherwise, I'm a pretty good person."

||||||||

THE WEEKS move faster with Angela around. She comes and goes, mostly on the weekends. Sometimes during the week. Roy doesn't mind. He wants to get on her about school, wants to make sure she goes. Does well. But he can't force her. If her mother doesn't argue, he won't. He hears about their arguments through Angela. Heather hasn't changed, hasn't changed a wink. If Angela doesn't leave on her own, she's thrown from the house until her mother calms down. He doesn't mind.

She's even taken to sprucing up his house a little. Brought in a few plants, taught him how to water them. How not to kill them. They name the plants together. Angela and Roy. One's a fern. One's a cactus.

And, despite his initial efforts to keep her out of the game, Roy finds himself teaching Angela some of what he knows. A few more games, here and there. During the downtime. He lets her run the twenties at 7-Elevens, her favorite target. She loves to play up to the clerks. Kids, adults, it doesn't matter. When Angela turns it on, Angela turns it on. Roy can't stand to watch. Roy can't stand not to watch. She's a natural.

Frankie doesn't come around as much as he used to. They still run games together, and they're still pulling the art deal. But he doesn't call for casual dinner. For drinks, whatever. At the diner, after business, they eat, they talk about the day, they go home. Roy doesn't tell Frankie about Angela, and Frankie doesn't ask about her. Two more times, they've played the Jamaican switch, and each time, Roy's left her at home. She pouted, of course, complained. No use.

Roy lets Angela keep whatever she earns on the C. Not fair to take the kid's money away. But he makes her promise to keep it secret from her mother. Wouldn't do good to have Heather on his ass again. She'd probably want in on it. Better to keep everything separate. Clean.

One night, a weeknight, when Angela has skipped her mother's house for the comforts of Roy's den once again, he helps her tidy up the room before heading out to meet Frankie. The watercolors have been taken off the walls. Most of them. In their place, more forgeries of forgeries: Mirós, Kandinskys, Wilders. Angela can't get enough of them. She loves the colors. The composition.

"Art's kinda a cool field," she tells him as they straighten out the bedsheets.

"You like that?" says Roy. "You should take some classes, some art classes."

Angela nods, thinking it over. "Might be cool. I could learn how to do that."

"Paint my portrait?"

"Only if I can sell it to you," she says. Roy laughs. Angela stands on the bed, running her fingers across the frame of a faux Rothko. "You got nice stuff in here now, Roy."

"Glad Her Majesty approves." It's easy talking to Angela these days. They get each other. She likes to tease, she's comfortable with that. He's comfortable with that, too.

"And as soon as you get rid of this ugly thing," she says, jumping off the bed and next to the ceramic horse, "we'll be set."

Roy freezes. "Don't mess with that. Forget it."

"It's ugly. Admit it."

"It was a gift."

"It's still ugly."

Her hands are all over the horse. Roy keeps himself even. He needs to make that Caymans trip. If he can make that trip, he'll never put money in that horse again. For now, it's hands off.

"Maybe it thinks you're ugly," he teases. "Maybe it wants to get rid of you."

Angela bites. "It's a statue, knucklehead."

"A statue that thinks you're ugly. Now get in bed, I gotta run out."

She hops back into the fold-out and pulls up the covers. "Deal with Frankie?"

"Yeah," he says. "I'd take you, but . . ."

"But he still doesn't like me. It's okay. Tell him I say hi."

"I will."

She flips on the black-and-white, the sound blasting into the room. "I'm sure there's something on the TV that can rot my brain."

"No doubt." Roy straightens his tie, tries to pull it up. Not having much success. Angela, exasperated, huffs theatrically and jumps to her knees, grabbing his tie with one hand and pulling it into place with the other. Leaps back down into the bed. Roy chuckles. "You want me to bring back ice cream or something?"

"Um . . . Rocky Road?"

"Rocky Road. Three hours, tops."

She turns the TV volume higher. "So go, already," she says. "Go on your date."

Roy closes the door behind him as he goes. Lets Angela have her privacy. She knows where to find things in the kitchen. Knows how to get around the house. He doesn't worry about leaving her at home anymore when he goes out. She's a big girl. She can take care of herself.

||||||||

THE ART dealer is located in the middle of an outdoor promenade. A busy shopping district. A happening store, a trendy store. A well-lit store. Roy doesn't like it. This is the kind of thing reserved for back-alley deals. The docks. The warehouse. And he doesn't understand why they have to make the drop themselves.

"I told you," Frankie says as they haul the crate out of the rented truck. "That guy, that friend of Jimmy's, he's sick tonight. He can't make the drop."

"It should wait," says Roy. No point in arguing. They're doing this thing already. "Next time, it can wait."

"I'm agreeing with you. But Saif said there's a flood coming his way from back East, and if we don't get this stuff on the market now, we'll lose out. Trust me, this guy wants to buy."

"You spoke with him?"

"I spoke with someone who spoke with him."

Always the intermediaries. It's safer, but a hell of a way to do business. Like playing that kid's game, Telephone. No way to know if what you're hearing is what you're supposed to be hearing. Roy's had it blow up in his face before.

But Frankie's right this time. The buyer is interested, and they unload four fakes on him at nine grand a pop, ten for the Corbett. The shop owner, who knows full well that these paintings are not the real thing, wants to take them out to dinner, to treat them to a nice meal, but Roy begs off. Doesn't want to make a thing of it. No need to socialize with the guy.

Afterward, he and Frankie walk the promenade. A slight chill comes down the street, whipping past the pedestrians. Roy likes it. It reminds him that winter's coming. No more fish guts at the docks.

Street performers line the edges of the stores. Singers, magicians. A guy who plays guitar and has his kid sing along. It's "Hotel California." It's always "Hotel California," every time he comes down here. That kid's been singing it since she was five. Roy shakes his head. To do that to a kid. To your own child. He drops a few coins in the guitar case.

"How's things?" Frankie asks.

"Good. You?"

"Good."

This isn't the kind of conversation they used to have. It used to be bright. Sometimes witty. Peppered with profanity, at the very least. Roy liked that. Frankie cursed better than anyone he'd ever met.

They pass through the nicer section of the promenade, leaving the upscale stores and restaurants behind. Now it's second-tier. Mom-and-pop operations, some empty storefronts. For Lease signs out in the window. Alleyways and dark corners. Roy's world. This is the kind of place where they should have brought the art. Things change.

As they turn the corner, Roy's surprised to see a throng of people gathered around. A three-quarter circle, those in back up on their toes. Roy knows that formation. That's a three-card-monte game. That's a street con going down. "Wanna check it out?" he asks Frankie. Doesn't need to wait for the response.

The young black man hustling the audience is making a good game of it. Letting the folks win when the bets are low, raking it back for himself when the money gets high. "Find the queen," he's saying, his hands moving over the cards. "Find the lady. The lucky lady is your friend."

Roy watches a few marks get taken for eighty, ninety bucks. The losers belly up and swim away, but the fringe crowd remains. They're not even in on it; they just want to see a skinning. Roy's feeling impetuous. He's feeling old school.

"I'll take a stab at it," he says, moving up to the table.

"Hey, hey, we got a player. What's your name, sir?"

"I'm Roy. From Des Moines." He's laying it on thick, he knows. Playing the chump. But this kid's too young to know any better.

"Roy from Des Moines, today could be your lucky day." The young man flips over the three cards on his table. Two aces, one queen in the middle. "Your job," he says, "is to find the queen. You find that beautiful, foxy lady, I double your money."

"Sounds easy. How much?"

"Let's call it twenty," says the kid. He picks up each card and puts it down again in succession. Picks it up, puts it down. Ace, queen, ace, queen, ace . . . Suddenly, there's a whirlwind of activity, the cards flying about the table. "Okay, where's the lady?"

This one isn't meant to be hard. Roy finds her easily. The kid pays out the money, and Roy slaps it back down. The cycle begins again. As he expected to, Roy wins the first few hands. Watches the cards, watches the kid's machinations. He needs work. His fingers are too stiff, the palms too loose. Good natural style, but he needs lessons. Roy's up sixty bucks when the hustler suggests they up the bet.

"How 'bout a hundred?" asks Roy, playing the cocky winner. The crowd oohs and aahs.

"A hundred it is," says the kid. Here's where Roy really pays attention. He knows he won't find the queen on the felt when the cards are all down. There won't be a queen. The kid will pocket the card, or palm it, or shove it up his sleeve, substituting a third ace. That's the trick to three-card-monte. There's no way to win.

Unless you're Roy. The kid throws down the cards, and Roy points to the middle one. Barely touches it. "You sure?" the kid asks.

"Sure enough to bet another hundred on it," says Roy. He lays down a second bill, and the kid, eager to suck in the country mouse, matches it. "Shake on the deal?" Roy asks, and before the kid can argue, Roy grabs his arm and pumps his hand hard.

The kid plays it off cool, smiling to the crowd. "So you want the lady in the middle?"

"Uh-huh. Can I flip it over?" Roy asks innocently.

"You can kiss it if you want."

Roy smiles and turns the card over. It's a queen. Roy wants a camera to capture the look on the kid's face. The crowd bursts into applause. Frankie snatches the money off the table and tucks it into Roy's jacket pocket. They quickly make their exit. No need to stick around. Hustlers like that don't like to lose. Hustlers like that don't like to be tricked at their own game.

"Nice switch," says Frankie. "I didn't even see it, and I knew it was coming."

"The kid's mechanics were lousy. He slipped that queen up

his sleeve, hell, I could see the white poking through. He didn't even notice I pulled it back out when we shook hands."

Frankie laughs. "Games on the hoof," he mutters. "Those were the old days, huh?"

"Bit takes, shaky payoffs, looking over your shoulder every two seconds, folding up if you caught a whiff of blue. Oh, yeah, real fun. Days of wine and roses."

"I dunno, I liked it. Easy, you know?" Roy doesn't want to admit it, but there are things about those days that he liked, too. Frankie's right—it was easier back then. No one suspecting you. No newsmagazines warning the public about the newest grift to hit the streets. These days it's all about shifty eyes. These days, some days, it's too much.

They turn the corner again, heading back to the car. The wind picks up. A couple sprints by in matching jogging shorts, huffing away. "How they walk around without jackets?" Frankie says. "It's fucking freezing out here."

"Reminds me. I gotta pick up some ice cream."

"I say it's freezing, he wants ice cream."

"Angela—she wanted some Rocky Road. There's a place back by the car, my treat."

They walk, huddling against the wind. Frankie pulls his jacket tight around his shoulders. Minutes pass in silence, Frankie glancing at Roy ever so often, as if waiting for the right moment to leap on his back or wrestle him playfully to the floor.

Eventually, he speaks. "So I had a little time on my hands. Thought up a new C."

"There are no new C's," says Roy. "It's all been done."

"I thought up a new *variation* then."

"Yeah?" Roy doesn't particularly care. The ones they've got

work well enough, and new material can be dangerous. But he doesn't want to upset his partner. Frankie's been testy enough recently. "Lay it out."

"Now, it's long con," he starts, "and I know that's not your bag—"

"Let's hear it. Go."

Frankie takes his hands from his pockets. Always talks with his fingers when he gets excited. "First of all, I'm talking a clean take from this. No wire hassles, nothing. Maybe fifty grand."

"Each?"

"Each."

A buzz in Roy's back pocket. The beeper. He pulls it out, checks the number. Unfamiliar. "Who is it?" Frankie asks.

"Dunno. Don't recognize it. Go on."

"Okay, easy setup. You seen these places, they buy out insurance policies from people who got AIDS?"

"I guess, yeah. Saw something on one of the news shows . . . They pay off a lump sum?"

"Right, right, that's it. Guy's dying from AIDS, he's got a million-dollar life insurance policy. These folks, they buy it out from him, give the guy a lump settlement like two hundred grand, then they get the million when he croaks."

The beeper goes off again, vibrating in Roy's hand. Same number as before, still unknown to him. It's certainly not Frankie, and Angela would have punched in Roy's home phone number. "Fucking kids," he mutters. Then, to Frankie: "Are you telling me you wanna run a scam on AIDS patients?"

"No, no. It don't gotta be AIDS, that's the beauty of this whole thing. Anybody got this situation going, this game will work. I mean, there's MS, the blacks have that sickle-cell thing . . ."

For the first time in weeks, Roy can taste the vomit in his throat. Starting low, almost down in his belly, climbing up like a steel worm, poking at his insides. The sting of acid in his mouth, saliva filling his cheeks. He spits, coughs, spits again. Frankie's still talking, talking about how they can split the proceeds after the insurance scam has been fixed up right.

The beeper, shaking his hand one more time. Vision is blurring, pulsing. The same number as before, and now he has to get to a phone. Just to get Frankie to stop talking. Get to a phone and call this number and whoever it is will help him. Will make the bile go away.

"Gotta call," Roy coughs, staggering across the street to a bank of pay phones. Frankie, confused, follows. Keeps up with his plan.

Roy throws his change down the slot and dials the phone number. Two rings, warbled. A pickup.

"Roy?" It's a voice he recognizes. A soothing voice. How did he know that Roy was in trouble? How did he know Roy needed to talk?

"Dr. Klein? Is that—"

"I'm sorry to page you like this," he says. "I didn't know if . . . I didn't really have a choice."

Roy doesn't understand, but he's glad to have the doc on the phone. Already the acid is sinking back down, canceling out. The saliva is drying up. "It's good. It's good. How . . . how are you?"

"I'm fine, Roy, but that's not why I called." His words are clipped. As if he's angry. "I'm calling about Angela."

"Angela? She's at my place."

A pause from the other end. Roy can hear muffled sobs in

the background. High-pitched sobs. “She’s not,” says Dr. Klein. “Not anymore.”

“What’s wrong? What happened?”

“She’s fine,” Klein assures him. “She’s fine now. A little upset, but . . . Come down here as soon as you can. You need to pick her up.”

“Where are you?” Dreading the answer. Almost knowing the answer.

“We’re at the police station, Roy. She’s had a long night, and I think she’d like to go home now.”

FOUR

THEY'RE SITTING on the front steps of the precinct when Roy and Frankie pull up to the station. Dr. Klein has his arm around Angela's shoulders, and she's fighting back the tears. Her cheeks are red, puffy, stained with salt water.

Roy leaps out of the rented truck, slamming the door behind him, jogging as fast as he can. Doesn't wait for Frankie to drag his ass out of the passenger seat. As he sprints for the steps, Angela looks up, sees him coming. Throws off Dr. Klein's arm and runs full bore at Roy, throwing herself into his arms. She's crying again, great heaving breaths feeding the tears.

"Shhh," says Roy, stroking her hair, "are you okay? Talk to me, are you okay?"

He feels motion against his chest. Her head, nodding. Not much, but nodding. Roy holds her closer. Moves with her sobs. Wants to wipe the tears away, make everything better. Erase time for her.

Klein approaches. "You got here quickly."

"What happened?"

"She got picked up." Dr. Klein sighs. "By the police."

Angela looks up at Roy, still wrapped in his arms. Her eyes are bloodshot, a thin layer of makeup running down her face in a muddy stream. She tries to speak through the sobs. "I didn't—I didn't know . . ." she starts, breaking down into a new fit.

Frankie saunters over, shaking his head. "She get booked?"

"Frankie," says Roy, "go sit in the car."

"What, I'm asking did she get booked, that's all."

Klein shakes his head. "No booking. No mug shot. They detained her, that's all."

Frankie nods his head. "Good. Lucky, but good."

Roy's arms tense around Angela, tightening his grip. If he doesn't hold on tight, he's liable to whip around, to let it all out. To grab Frankie by the neck, to strangle out the air. To make him blue. Silence him that way if need be. "Frankie," he says again, trying to control every syllable. "Go sit in the car or shut up."

Frankie backs off. Sits himself down on the edge of a concrete planter and watches the scene.

Angela is calming down again, trying to speak. "They . . . they put me in a cell. With all these people. These . . . these women, but they were . . . They kept touching me. They kept trying to . . ." The words coming harder suddenly, the gasps increasing, ". . . to touch me . . ." And she's off again, crying uncontrollably into Roy's shirt.

"It was tough in there," Dr. Klein says. "They had her for at least an hour, in there with a group of prostitutes they'd picked up. I don't know what happened, but she was screaming when I got here, barely recognized me. She's had a rough night."

"You shoulda paged me," Roy says, stroking her hair, her back, anything to calm her down. "Hon, you shoulda paged me right off."

"She didn't know your pager number. And until she thought to look me up in the phone book . . . Lucky I was working late."

"Doc," he says, "I can't thank you enough. I mean . . ." He doesn't know how to handle this. Doesn't know the etiquette when your daughter's been picked up by the cops and your shrink headed down to spring her. "Whatever I can do for you . . ."

Klein shakes his head. "Nothing. Glad I could help, that's all."

Frankie's back off the planter. "She get fingerprinted?" he asks the doctor.

"That ain't our concern," Roy says.

"It's my concern."

"No," the doctor cuts in. "Like I said, just detained. No record of anything."

Angela breaks away from Roy, wiping her face with her sleeve. "I . . . I tried the lottery game," she whimpers. "I was trying it out, like you . . . like we talked about . . ."

Frankie throws his arms in the air, shaking his head. "What the fuck? You're schooling her on *games* now, Roy?"

It's all moving fast. Roy doesn't want Klein here for this. He doesn't want Angela here. He wants it all to go away. "Frankie, keep your fucking mouth shut."

And Angela's still trying to explain. "And I guess . . . I guess the lady, I didn't know she was a cop . . ."

"Shh," Roy says, trying to draw her near again. "It's okay, it's all over."

"Too fucking much," mutters Frankie.

"Excuse me?"

"Too fucking much."

Klein tries to step in. "Fellas, it's late. It's late, and we're outside the precinct, and I think it's just better if—"

Roy pushes Klein aside. "Frankie, you'll shut up if you know what's good for you."

"Oh, fuck you, Roy. You know what? Fuck you."

"You wanna say that again?"

"You heard me, you fat motherfucker. Fuck. You."

Angela's tears are new now, a fresh crying jag. She backs away from Roy and Frankie as they come closer to one another. Roy's vision blurring, the delicious pressure hitting him in the temples. Pulsing.

"This is . . . Let's calm down. Everyone needs to take a moment's breath," suggests Dr. Klein.

No takers. Roy and Frankie are a foot apart and closing. "Why don't you kiss her, Roy?" says Frankie.

"Shut up, Frankie."

"Grab her close, kiss her like you know you want to."

"Shut up. Frankie."

"Take her home to your bed—"

"You got two seconds to close that mouth—"

"—lay her down, kiss her all over—"

"—or I'm gonna shut it for you."

Frankie narrows his eyes. "What's the problem, Roy? Not man enough to screw your own daughter?"

It's like the barroom fight, like the time he got discharged from the army. It's a halo of light around Frankie's head, a giant lightbulb flipped on in the sky. Blinding, powerful. Explosions in

Roy's skull, like his brain expanding, popping out. No thoughts. No thoughts.

A fist rises through the air, slamming down onto Frankie's head, crushing his cheek with a powerful blow. Another, raining into his midsection, tumbling him over as he rushes for Roy. The two go down in a heap, rolling along the cracked pavement. Tumbling down the stairs, limbs locked, Roy's head slamming into the concrete. Doesn't feel a thing. The pressure is good, the pressure is what he needs. Frankie's nose, bleeding out, bleeding strong. Blood on Roy's hands. The light subsiding. It's good. It's right.

Somebody, screaming in the background. Some voice Roy recognizes, something he should listen to. But his body continues with the beating, with the punches and the kicks, hard bones into soft flesh. Another scream, this one closer, breaking through. Hands on his shoulders, pulling him back, pulling him away. The pressure folding down. The light fading back into night.

"Stop it!" Angela is screaming. "Stop it!"

Klein, pulling Roy away from Frankie, trying to lift his body off the smaller man. Trying to save his life. The halo clearing. The picture swimming back into focus. Roy rolls himself off his partner, onto the ground.

"Get out of here," Klein says to Roy, helping him to his knees before attending to Frankie. "Go, take the girl."

A hundred feet away, up by the precinct door, a uniformed officer looks down at the scuffling pair. "There a problem down there?" he calls.

"No problem," Klein calls back. "We'll be getting out of the way, Officer."

The cop doesn't move as Klein helps Frankie to his feet. His nose is bloodied, his lips cracked. Bruises are already forming beneath both eyes. His voice is low, morose. Deflated of his earlier bravado. "You call me when you got your priorities screwed on straight," he says to Roy, staggering off toward the truck. Turns to Angela, points a finger at her face. "And you . . . you go back to your fucking dolls."

They watch as he stumbles into the truck and guns the engine. The tires squeal as he shoots down the road, taillights fading into the distance.

Angela slowly shuffles up to Roy, staring down at her feet. "Are you mad at me?" she asks.

He's too tired to speak. Can barely get the words out. "No, hon."

She hugs him tight, her arms a belt around his waist. Stays there. "I pulled off a few twenties before I got busted," she says.

"That's good, hon. That's good."

Dr. Klein drives them home that night. Roy doesn't know how it happens, but by the time he's come back to conscious thought, his face is clean, he's changed into his nightclothes, and he's lying down in bed with the covers pulled up tight. He hopes Angela is sleeping. Can't think about what he needs to do. Knows what that thing is, but can't think about it right now. In the morning, it will all make sense. In the morning, everything will be all right. It always is. It always used to be.

|||||||||

PLATFORM D is filled with travelers heading out into the heart of the country. All types mill around, waiting for their train to arrive, and Roy fights the urge to fix any of them up with a con.

He's got Angela by the hand. Doesn't want his thoughts corrupting hers. Not anymore.

"Thanks for coming in with me," she says.

"Yeah, well . . . I got nowhere to be."

"First time in here?"

Roy nods. "I used to take buses. Never been on a train."

Angela smiles. "You can come with me. See my mom and get in a life experience all at the same time."

Roy shakes his head. "I don't think that'd be a good idea. All around."

"Can't hurt to try."

"Sometimes it can." Roy looks down at Angela's ticket. The train will be leaving in a few minutes.

Angela hikes her duffel bag onto her shoulder. "So when am I coming back?" she asks. She's been like this all morning, full of questions. Roy's been evading them as best as he can. "Next week?"

"We'll play it by ear," Roy says. "I'm sure your ma wants to see you some, too. You been out here an awful lot."

"Yeah, I guess. And there's school."

"Right. You gotta go to school."

They walk toward the train in silence, Angela grasping onto Roy's hand. She stops, looks up at him, a tear welling in the corner of her eye. Ready to drop. "If this is because of the other night—"

"No, no, it's not—"

"—I can make it right again. I can make it better, I swear I'll make it better."

Roy's shaking his head. Doesn't know if it's more for Angela or for himself. "It's not . . . That's got nothing to do with it." He crouches down, coming to her eye level. His quadriceps shaking under the pressure. "I ain't too good with new things. I've never really been able to . . . adjust. Most times, I need stability."

"I can be stable."

"What I'm saying is, I got used to having you around. You're part of . . . you know, you're part of it now. And that's great. That's better than great."

"So what's the problem?"

"There's no problem, hon," he says. But he doesn't want to lie to her. Not now. "It's just . . . I gotta take stock, that's all. See where I am right now. See where I wanna be. That's what Doc Klein says, at least. You understand?"

"Not really."

"Me either." He laughs. Straightens up, his legs protesting. "C'mon, don't miss your train."

Roy grabs Angela and lifts her onto the train, duffel bag and all. She's not crying now, not really, and Roy is glad for it. "When I come back," she says, "we'll watch the late show?"

"All the way to the end," he promises.

Angela leans down from inside the train, one hand grabbing the rail to steady herself, and plants a kiss on Roy's cheek. "Bye, Dad," she whispers.

By the time Roy looks up, she's gone. A few moments later, the train is, too.

||||||||

THE MAIN airport on Grand Cayman is sixteen miles outside of George Town. The cab ride into the city is smooth enough, but the cabbie's air is out, so they roll along with the windows down.

Roy doesn't mind. The wind feels good against his forehead. He hates planes, hates being stuck in a seat for that long. Even a big seat. He always springs for first class. Doesn't think of it as a luxury. It's a necessity. Coach would kill him. No exaggeration, Roy thinks. Kill him.

The back of the cab jumps wildly with every pothole. It's weighted down with Roy's luggage. Three bags in all, large suitcases with extra security padlocks. Each bag contains approximately two hundred thousand dollars in American currency. Money that used to be holed up in the ceramic horse. Soon, it will be safely in Roy's numbered account at the Grand National Bank in George Town. For now, he worries about it. What if the cab hits a hard bump? What if the trunk opens up? What if the bags go flying out? What if they crack open on a rock? That sort of thing.

Wouldn't be happening if he'd remembered his pills. Left them on the kitchen counter. Roy can see where they are, picture the bottle next to the coffeemaker. He's been thinking about them since the plane took off. Since it was too late. Like his brain was playing a joke on him, keeping it a secret until he was airborne. He would have gotten off the plane if it was still on the ground. Considered making a fuss, getting them to land again, but knew it was more trouble than it was worth.

He called Klein as soon as he landed on Grand Cayman, and the doctor said that missing a few days' worth of pills wouldn't do anything to his condition. That it was not a problem, that he should relax. The Caymans are an island paradise, the doctor said. Roy didn't tell him he was down here on business. No need for the doctor to know that. He probably knew too much already.

The taxi eventually makes its way into the heart of the city, and Roy gives the driver instructions to wait for him outside the bank. It can be hell trying to pick up a cab at the wrong time in George Town, and he doesn't want to wait on the street for hours. Wants to check in at his hotel, find something to eat. Sleep.

Roy doesn't want to be conspicuous dragging his luggage inside the bank, but it's difficult to manage the three bags at once. He manages to haul them inside the entrance, then waits. Stands there with a purposeful look on his face, and waits. This is not the first time Roy's done this. He knows it will work.

The female teller who comes over is a new face, but Roy knows his main contacts will still be around. "Can I help you with that, sir?"

"Mr. Cheively, please. Is he around?"

She nods and asks Roy to wait but a second. He looks around the bank, at the other customers. He's not the only one with luggage. With bags too heavy for clothing. He's not the only one who's keeping his guard up.

Roy hears his name called out, and he looks up to find Mr. Cheively, his usual contact. "You did not call to say you were coming," says the bank executive in the clipped British tones Roy has come to expect from the Cayman natives. "I would have arranged for accommodations."

"I didn't want to bother anyone," says Roy. He never calls ahead. He knows that if he does, Cheively will try to get him to go to dinner, to set him up with a ladyfriend of his, that sort of thing. It had happened before, at the old bank. A Cayman way of encouraging their clientele. Roy doesn't need encouragement. The anonymous bank accounts and offshore protection are all he cares about.

After a few more blandishments, Cheively takes Roy into the back, helping to drag the suitcases with him. They total the money up together, the executive working a large, old-fashioned calculator to add up the sums. "Are we adding this to the main account, or starting a new one?"

"Same account," says Roy. He's never seen the point of spreading the money out. Hidden cash is hidden cash. One bundle, ten bundles, it's all the same thing. More numbers to remember that way. More passwords. Hassle.

After the cash is counted, after the final amount is tallied and agreed upon, Roy and Mr. Cheively go through the motions of accessing the account. Though Mr. Cheively knows that Roy is, indeed, the holder of the Grand National Bank account, he is duty-bound to get both the numbers and the designated password from him. These are the only things required to access the account, Roy knows. This is why he keeps this information solely in his mind. Not written down, anywhere. Once upon a time, he had the numbers scattered across his house, coded down inside a Rolodex listing. But he tore those up. Security risk. It's in his brain, or it's nowhere.

"So now I've got . . . what?"

Mr. Cheively gives Roy a figure that hovers just above the four-million-dollar mark. He's satisfied. That's what he expected.

"Now," says the British banker, "is there anything else I can do for you? Food, drink . . . women?"

Roy shakes his head, pumps the man's hand. "I'll be fine. I fly back tomorrow."

The cabdriver is waiting outside, and Roy climbs in. "Hyatt Villas," he says. "Wake me when we get there." Roy settles down in the back of the cab, tucking his legs under him for the drive to Seven-Mile Beach. He's glad to be rid of the cash, to get it out of the horse, out of his house. Into safety. He tries to sleep as the taxi bounces across the road, the wind whipping through his hair. Traffic begins to intensify as they near the resort. Tourists in their own cabs, in their own rental cars, shooting by, clogging up the main resort arteries. Roy remembers when he first started coming here, almost ten years back. When it wasn't so crowded. When his suitcases weren't so heavy.

Roy's suite isn't ready yet. It's after three, after check-in time, but the room isn't prepared. He'd put up a fuss, growl, complain, but there's no point. He's not really upset. Highsmith, the hotel manager, feels bad enough to comp him in the lounge. Wanted to get some sleep, but a drink will do.

The lounge is empty this afternoon, just a few couples slumped in the overstuffed chairs, staring out at the sea. Big picture windows with majestic views of the ocean. Roy's seen it. It's blue. It's wet. He doesn't know how to scuba. Doesn't want to snorkel. He sits at the bar, his back to the water.

"What can I get you?" asks the bartender.

"Gin and tonic, twist," says Roy. "Highsmith sent me."

The bartender doffs a hat that's not there and mixes up Roy's drink. "Enjoying your stay, sir?"

"Just started it, friend." Roy grabs at a bowl of almonds and cracks them between his teeth.

The bartender squeezes a quarter of lime into Roy's drink. Slides it across the bar. "Do you plan on enjoying your stay, then?"

"Preferably," says Roy.

"Family?"

"No," says Roy instinctively. Then, almost as quickly: "A daughter. Back in the States. She's fourteen."

The bartender smiles and grabs an almond of his own. Casual fellow. "You should bring her next time. We've got a lot for a young girl to do. She like to go diving?"

"I don't know," says Roy.

"Swimming? Snorkeling? Volleyball?"

He shakes his head again. "Not sure."

The bartender cocks his head. "What does she like, then? I'm sure we have it."

"We played games. We always liked to play games." He sucks down a gulp of his drink. It tastes bitter.

The bartender spreads his arms wide. "We got all kinda games around here. We got a whole room full of 'em. She like chess? We got a beautiful room with chessboards, looks out right over the water. . . ."

Roy leaves the bartender talking to himself. Stands up and strolls to the edge of the lounge. The picture window in front of him, the glass walls to the hotel. He can almost see his reflection, at the same time as he's looking out on the ocean. Like he's on top of the water. Like he's inside the water. Like it's surrounding him, comforting him, buoying him. The ground below his feet, blue and wet, the carpet soaked and wet. The carpet. Wet.

Roy looks down. He's spilled his drink. All over the carpet, he's spilled his drink. A dark stain spreads across the thick white pile of the lounge. Stained, he thinks. Permanently stained. Now the ocean is closing in. Pushing, from all sides. His legs wobble, begin to buckle beneath his body. He takes a seat in a nearby chair, arms dangling from the sides. Head back, propped so he can see the sunset. He's seen it before, of course. It's pink. It's yellow. It's blue. It's all those things, but it's better than watching the carpet. Better than watching the stain, which is spreading even now, spreading across the whole floor. A permanent discoloration. Filthy. Ruined.

And the bile begins to rise again. Roy curses himself silently. This is stupid, this is wrong. Klein said this wouldn't happen. He said the pills wouldn't work this way, that they'd stay in his body. But the bile is coming fast, and he can picture it. Green, slimy, crawling up his throat. Slowly, like a horror movie monster. Tickling his uvula. Filling his mouth with saliva. The carpet below, stained. Ready to be stained more. Ready to be destroyed.

He bursts from the lounge, stumbling into the lobby. Slamming into tourists. Shocked gasps. Wide eyes. Running to the rest rooms out front. Falling into a stall, onto his knees, tearing his pants. Pulling the bowl wide, stomach coming up, coming out. Mouth spreading, allowing for the flow, ready for the onslaught.

Nothing. Dry heaves again. Small hacks, coughs. Cackles. His shoulders shaking with each convulsion. Tears dropping into the bowl. Running down his cheeks. Breath coming sharp, cool air running into his throat. The stinging gone now. The bile gone now. The carpet, gone.

Roy staggers to his feet, out of the stall. Washes off his face. Straightens his tie. Wipes down his scraped knees. They'd better have his room ready now. They'd better give him one with hardwood floors.

||||||||

STOP SIGNS are not Roy's concern as he makes his way back home. Traffic signals are disregarded. It's all about speed. It's all about shortcuts. Roy is at the tail end of a sleepless night and day. He maneuvers his car in a half-fog, keeping his eyes on the road as best he can. This morning, he barely made it out of the hotel in time to catch his plane. Checked the room to make sure he didn't leave anything, then checked it again. And again. Six run-throughs before he was convinced, then he closed the door. Thought it was over. An hour later, he had checked it five more times.

He knows he's in trouble. Knows he needs to get at that medicine. Called Klein from the airport, but he wasn't in. Machine picked up. Roy figures he'll call once he's at home, once he's taken the pills. The pills are waiting for him there.

The flight back was an exercise in self-control. In breathing patterns. In keeping his eyes closed. One of the pretty little stewardesses nearly went home with a broken nose. She kept trying to wake Roy during the flight. To offer him cocktails. To tell him about the movie. To suggest he buckle his safety belt. The last time, Roy didn't even look up. He let his hand fly through the air, narrowly missing her face by an inch. She didn't bother him again.

Roy pulls onto his block, into the driveway. Relieved to be home. Exhausted, but elated. The pills are inside, just in the kitchen. He fumbles with the lock, then slaps himself awake. One strong hand across the cheek. He's up.

He steps inside, closes the door. Locks it. Tries to walk away, but suddenly thinks that he may not have locked it far enough. Unlocks the door, then locks it back up again. Watches the bolt sliding into the frame. That should be good. That should be enough. Roy takes a deep breath and turns his back on the front door. Steps away.

Five paces, six paces. One by one, into the kitchen. He turns the corner, ready to end all of this nonsense, ready to get back to normalcy. Expecting to find salvation next to the coffee machine.

It's not there. The pill bottle isn't there. And Roy knows what's about to come: the bile, the stinging. The vomit.

It all passes. Next to the refrigerator, the bottle. His bottle. His pills. Not where he remembers leaving them, but it doesn't matter. Roy rushes for the drugs, catching the bottle up in one hand as he fills a water glass with the other. He needs a double shot, a triple shot. Anything. He pops the container.

One pill left. Roy blinks. Sticks his finger into the bottle, twisting it around. One pill. Shakes the container up and down, as if one might be stuck inside the plastic and needs to be jarred loose. One pill. Has he run out that quickly? Is he that low? This won't do. If he takes that last pill, then he'll have none. No pills for tonight. No pills for tomorrow. This won't do at all.

He's on the phone seconds later, dialing Klein's number. The phone rings, rings again. A pickup.

"Doc," he blurts out, "I need more of that Effexor."

"You've reached the medical group's answering service," comes the polite female voice on the other end of the line. "The doctors aren't in right now."

Roy looks at his watch; it's past seven. "You gotta patch me through," he says. "I'm calling for Dr. Klein. Harris Klein. I'm a patient."

"This is Dr. Klein's answering service," she repeats. "I can send him a message, if you would like."

"A message—no, that's not gonna help. Look, I gotta talk to him now."

"Sir, I can send him a message, but I don't have a direct line for the doctor."

Roy grabs the phone handset tighter, pressing it into his ear. "I need . . . look, look, let's be reasonable. I can be reasonable, can you?"

"Sir—"

"Good. I need a new bottle of pills. That's all. It's the same pills I've been taking for months, and the doctor gives 'em to—"

She cuts in. "If you've got a prescription, any pharmacy—"

"I don't have one, I just have—look, he gave me the pills, okay? Dr. Klein, he gave me the pills, and I need to . . ." Roy stops. Thinks. "Are you at the office?"

"No, sir. I'm at a central answering station."

"Uh-huh. But you can get into the office. If you have to."

"Sir, I—"

"If you have to."

A sigh from the other end. "In emergencies, yes, sir, but—"

"This *is* an emergency!" Roy shouts into the phone. He never raises his voice, prides himself on it. Doesn't care now. "I need these pills—"

"I understand, but—"

"—to function. I need them to *function.* I'll buy you dinner, okay? I'll buy you a fucking car. Just get me a bottle of what I need."

There's a pause on the other end. Is she considering it? Roy holds his breath. "Sir, I can leave the doctor a message—"

He slams the phone onto the countertop, wielding the handset like a club. Plastic splintering, breaking off. Shards flying about the kitchen. Roy doesn't notice, doesn't care. Bashing that voice into submission, shutting up that goddamned woman. Shutting up the whole goddamned world.

||||||||

THE LIGHTS inside the drugstore are bright. Roy fumbles inside his coat for the sunglasses. Throws them on, shading his eyes. It's better. Still bright, but better. This is the closest drugstore he could find. The closest he could think of. It was hard to get out of the house. It was hard to get that goddamned front door locked up right.

He's got the bottle in his pocket. One pill left. Doesn't want to take it. Doesn't want to take it until he knows there's more on the way. Can't be empty. Empty would be a travesty. Empty would be a hazard.

It's a big place. Discount drugstore. Aisles and aisles, not just medicine. Household cleaning supplies. Food. Drinks. Clothing. Books. Appliances. Ice cream, for chrissakes. Ice cream in a drugstore. He doesn't understand why they would do that.

"Where's the pharmacy?" he asks the first employee he sees.

The boy doesn't hear Roy's mumble. "Wha?"

"The fucking pharmacy," snaps Roy. "Where is it?"

It's in the back. Way in the corner. Roy makes his way through the aisles, brushing past the other customers. Shouldering them aside. They don't get out of his way quickly enough. They don't know how to move. They're sheep, all of them. A herd of sheep.

There's a line, snaking around. A rope, set up to maintain that line. One fellow at the desk. White coat. White hair. Must be the pharmacist. That's the guy he needs to see. The man with the key.

Five people in front of him. Woman with a baby over her shoulder. It's gurgling. Trying to talk. Looking at Roy's glasses, at its own reflection. Two men in front of her. They look healthy, Roy thinks. What the hell do they need the pharmacy for?

Up front, an older woman is talking with the pharmacist. Roy can't hear their conversation, but it looks casual. Worse than that, it looks nonmedical. Like she's already been given her drugs, and they're just talking about the day's events.

"Move along, lady," Roy calls out. The other customers look at him. He looks right back. They wisely look away.

The longer Roy waits, the more he thinks about his pills. That they're right there, twenty feet away, somewhere up on those shelves. That it will just take that little man right there to go back and get them. Grab a bottle, pass it over. If it weren't for all these people in the way. Healthy people. People who don't need to be here.

The old woman finally moves out of the way, but Roy can't take it anymore. He scoots out of the line and hustles up to the front counter, shoving aside the middle-aged fellow at the front.

"Hey, buddy," the guy says, "there's a line here."

"Emergency," Roy mutters.

"Yeah, we all got emergencies, friend," says the man. He's standing tall, standing tough. Comes an inch or two higher than Roy. Looking down on him.

Roy tries to smile. To grin at the man. To handle this properly. "I'm in a bit of a pickle . . . *friend.* Maybe you could help me out."

"And maybe you could go back to the end of the line." He places a hand on Roy's shoulder, exerting pressure. Trying to send him back.

Roy clamps his own hand down atop the man's, lifts his other arm into the elbow pit. He bends, twists, and the man is soon down on his knees, his arm caught up in Roy's, his face set in a mask of blazing pain. Whimpering. Mewling.

The pharmacist is aghast. "What are you—let him go—"

"I'll be outta everyone's way in ten seconds," Roy announces.

"Sir, there's a line—"

"I *know* there's a line. I *see* the line. My eyesight's not the problem. I see the line." Roy drops the man's arm; he scoots backward, away from Roy's reach. "Look, I'm not . . . *myself* today. I need help." He reaches into his pocket. Pulls out the bottle of pills, plops it down on the counter. "I need a refill."

The pharmacist wants to get this over with quickly. Looks to the other customers. They also want this over with quickly. Fine. Good. He picks up the bottle, looks at the label. "This isn't from our store."

"I know that," says Roy. "I know that."

"Do you have a prescription?"

"My doc—Dr. Klein—he gave me the pills. He—after the session, he gives me the pills, you know? I thought I had more, but—"

"I'm sorry," says the pharmacist. "I can't help you without a prescription. It's the law."

Roy snatches the bottle from the man's hand, points to the label. "Look here," he says. "Effexor. It says it, right there. Effexor, one hundred milligrams. And that's my name, right next to it. I'm Roy. That's me."

The pharmacist shakes his head. "I see that, but . . . I can't help you, sir."

Roy stops. Takes a breath. Doesn't want this to get out of control. He's composed himself well so far. Klein would be proud. Roy wrestles with the pop top, twisting the bottle open. Inside is a familiar green pill. Roy shakes it into his hand, holds it out for the pharmacist to see.

"See this? Effexor. See, I've got a pill already. So clearly I'm allowed to have them."

The pharmacist looks across the drugstore, toward one of his assistants. She nods and picks up the phone. "Without a prescription," he repeats, "I can't be of help."

"Please," says Roy, his ire rising. "I don't beg. I've never begged. But I'm begging you. Nine, ten of these. To cover the weekend. Until my shrink gets back."

From the front of the drugstore, two hired security guards begin to make their way toward the pharmacy. Toward the commotion. They hustle down the aisles.

"Without a prescription—"

"Goddamn it!" Roy shouts. "Goddamn you people! I've got Effexor here. Right here, and all I'm asking for is a little more!"

The pharmacist is about to repeat his stock phrase again when the pill catches his eye. Green. It's green, but the shouting man thinks it's Effexor. "Let me see that," says the pharmacist, picking the pill up between his thumb and forefinger. Holding it toward the light.

"Thank you," Roy says. Nearly breaking down. Out of relief. Of gratitude. "Thank you."

The pharmacist shakes his head. "This isn't Effexor," he says.

Roy doesn't hear him properly. "Excuse me?"

"This isn't Effexor. It's not an antidepressant at all."

Roy shakes his head. He doesn't understand. That's what Klein had been giving him. Antidepressants for the compulsions. For the . . . for his problems. What the hell is this guy talking about? "What—what is it?"

"I don't know," says the pharmacist. "But it's not Effexor. Effexor comes in tablets and capsules, but they're bluish, not green like this." The security guards move quickly down the aisle, heading for Roy, for the large flailing man up front. The one with the delusions. The fits.

Roy grabs the pill back, staring at it. Trying to see inside. He twists the top half of the capsule, popping it off the bottom. Spills out the white powder within, spreading it across the pharmacist's desk. "So what is it?" he asks. "What is it, if it's not Effexor?"

The pharmacist takes a good look. Notices the granules. The familiar white sheen to the powder. He dips a finger inside and licks the tip. "It's sugar," he says plainly. "Your doctor's been giving you sugar pills."

Roy doesn't wait for the security guards to grab his arms. Doesn't wait to be led away. There's no warning this time, no tickling at the back of the throat. No sudden sensation of pressure. Roy vomits right there. Right on the pharmacist's desk. On the pharmacist. On the other customers. He vomits, and he vomits, and he vomits, and he collapses in a heap on the floor of the discount drugstore.

THREE

THE SECRETARY tries to stop Roy as he barges into the office, but she's too slow. Can't get out from behind her desk. He throws open the lobby door and storms down the paneled hallway. Klein's office door is closed. Roy doesn't care. Roy doesn't care if it's locked. He'll break it down. He'll break it off the hinges if he has to.

He hasn't washed this morning. He hasn't shaved since the day before he headed out to Grand Cayman. Last night, Roy didn't sleep. He staggered out of the drugstore and into his car. Spent most of the evening going from bar to bar, trying to order drinks. Noticing all the crud on the floors. On the walls. On the glasses they tried to serve him. Throwing them down, throwing them away. Waiting for nine in the morning to roll around. Waiting to confront Klein. He fell asleep around six-thirty in the bathroom stall of an all-night club, waking up at ten. Washing his face in the sink. Washing his hands. Washing them again.

The door slams hard into the wall as Roy throws it open, the doorknob smashing into the plaster. He stands there, in the doorway, taking up the whole frame. Secretary running behind him, trying to catch up, trying to shout her apologies.

Inside, Klein is at his desk, deep in conversation with another man sitting in the patient's chair. He looks up, startled, as the door flies in. Eyes wide, shocked as he sees Roy enter. Backing up. "It's okay, Wanda," he tells the receptionist. "I can handle it." Reluctantly, she slinks back to her desk.

Roy's across the room in two bounding steps, anger carrying his bulky frame. "Sugar pills?" he yells, throwing the bottle at Klein. Hitting him in the chest. "You gave me fucking sugar pills?"

He's at the doctor's side. Hands an inch from his face. Klein tries to scoot backward, his chair caught in the carpeting. Tipping back. "Roy, this isn't a good time."

"I got a chemical malfunction, you know that?"

"Please, Roy—"

"I got a chemical malfunction *in my brain.* I need the right drugs, the right class of medicine. Not some fucking sugar pills!" He's leaning in farther now, dancing with the doctor. Klein moves back, Roy moves forward. Not controlling his own motions. Not thinking about them. "What am I, a fucking test case for you? A guinea pig for some fucking paper you're writing?"

The doctor motions to his patient, who is still sitting peacefully in the chair. Eyes half closed, a bemused smile on his face. "I've got a patient here."

"And what am I? Huh? Don't I pay you?"

"We can discuss this in an hour—"

"We can discuss this now." Roy looks over to the other patient and waves his hand. "Scram, I gotta talk to the doc."

There's no response. Not even the hint of movement. A touch of a smile still riding those lips. "The fuck is wrong with him?"

"He's under hypnosis," says Klein. "I can't send him out of the room as long as he's still under. I'm sorry."

Roy circles the desk, peering at the other man. Bends down to take a look at his eyes. At that smile. Roy grabs the patient by the shoulders and shakes him violently, his neck snapping around. "Wake up!" he yells in the young man's ears. Slaps him across the face. "Wake the fuck up!"

The patient startles to consciousness, eyes blinking. Looking around in a fog. "What . . ."

"Hey, you still sleeping?"

"No . . . no, I don't think—"

"Good," says Roy, hauling the guy onto his feet. "Good-bye." He ushers the patient out of the office, slamming the door closed behind him.

"That was unprofessional, Roy," says Klein.

Roy laughs. Lets out a good one. "You're a funny man, doc. You're gonna talk to me about professionalism." Walks back to the desk, perches on the edge. Legs kicking out, brushing Klein's knee. "So, you wanna explain yourself?"

"Do you want to sit down?"

"I am."

"Like a . . . like a patient? In the chair?"

Roy hops off the desk and grabs the chair by the seat, pulling it out and around the table. Next to Klein's. A foot away. He sits. Stares. Doesn't want the doctor too far. Doesn't want him comfortable. "How's this?"

"It's—fine. Roy, why do you think you need the pills?"

Roy shakes his head, bottom lip pursed out. "No, no, no. You're not asking the questions yet. First you answer. Did you give me sugar pills?"

"Yes."

"Okay, then." He didn't expect it that easily. Expected a fight. "Why?"

"Because you don't need the Effexor."

"Fuck that. I have a chemical—"

"Malfunction, I know. In your brain, I know, I know. Listen to me for a second, and we can work this out. You tell me: Why do you think you need the pills?"

Roy lifts his hands. They're shaking. Trembling. Been that way since last night. Since the drugstore. "Look at me," he says. "I'm a fucking wreck."

"Agreed."

"I can't—I can't think straight, I'm not . . . acting right. My mouth, it's all filled with spit all the time. I can't walk out of a room without checking the door—without locking it and locking it again. I can't look at the carpet, at the fibers. I got this, this pain in my throat, this liquid, it stings, it makes me sick. I almost got arrested at the drugstore last night. You want more?"

"And you attribute this to my giving you the sugar pills."

"You did."

"I did."

Roy spreads his hands wide. "This is what I'm saying. Sugar pills, I lose it. What more is there?"

Klein sits back. Roy doesn't pursue. "How's Angela?" he asks.

Roy coughs. "Don't change the subject."

"This is the subject. How's Angela?"

"She left."

"When?"

"Last week," Roy says.

"What day?"

"I dunno. Tuesday, Wednesday. A few days before my trip."

Klein nods. Grabs that damned notepad. Roy snatches it up and throws it across the room. It slams into a wall and falls to the floor.

Dr. Klein puts his pencil on the desk, but otherwise doesn't seem startled. As if he expected it from Roy, a move like that. "So she's been gone . . . how long?"

"Six, seven days."

"Uh-huh. Seven days."

Roy balls his fists. He's not going to hit the doctor, not yet, but it feels good to have them tight like that. "You got a point here?"

"Have you talked to her since she left?"

Roy shrugs. "She's got school—"

"So you haven't."

"No, but she's got stuff to do. What, am I supposed to track her down? She'll call me when she calls me."

"You haven't tried to call her."

"No. It's . . . better. This way. She's gotta be with her mom."

Klein looks up. "Are you starting to see this, yet?"

"What?"

"The correlation. Angela leaving and your . . . difficulties."

Roy shakes his head. Doesn't get it. Shrink trick, that's all it is. "Doc, you gave me sugar pills. That's the correlation."

"So you don't see it."

"Don't do this." Roy sighs. Knows he's at a loss. His edge gone. "What? What don't I see?"

Klein scoots his chair forward, his knees touching Roy's. He couldn't get any closer without a kiss. "I had a patient," he begins. "Three, four years back. Good guy, in general. Loved his family, loved his friends, would do anything for them. And things didn't always go well for him. Life took its toll, like it does on all of us. Most people accept and move on. But he had what we call an attribution deficiency."

"Lost me."

"Fancy way of saying he laid off blame. For example: In college, he failed an astronomy class. He decided it was because the professor had it in for him. Didn't like him from day one."

"Maybe so," says Roy.

"Maybe. But it became a pattern. He got fired from work. Three different jobs. Why? Each time, he said it was because his supervisor didn't like his hair, his clothes, his whatever. Eventually, his wife left him. Why? Well, she must have had commitment issues. It couldn't have been anything *he* did. One night, his house burned down because he fell asleep in his easy chair with a cigarette in his hand. What did he do? He sued the tobacco company and the store where he bought the pack of cigarettes." Roy can't help but laugh a little; Klein joins in. "This sounding familiar, Roy?"

"You're saying I should blame myself?"

"I'm saying you're looking in the wrong place, that's all. I'm saying you're looking to blame the pills, when that's not the answer. I've had you on sugar pills since the first day you came to see me—"

"You son of a bitch—"

"—and by your own admission, you were doing great. You came in here that third, fourth week, couldn't be better. The obsessive/compulsive loop had calmed down, the depression had subsided, and by the second month of treatment, you were as up as you've ever been. Practically danced in here on a cloud that one day. Said so yourself."

Roy can't deny it. Wants to, but can't. "Yeah. So?"

"So the point is, you don't need any Effexor. I could prescribe it to you right now. Take out my pad and write you up a scrip, and you'd be living it up at the local pharmacy in no time. But I won't, because you don't need it. It's been months now since you've been taking those sugar pills, and if you didn't run out, if you didn't go to the pharmacy, you never would have known the difference. So what's the problem? What's the reason you're really starting to lose it again?"

Roy knows the answer. Doesn't want to say it yet. Klein doesn't mind waiting. They stare at each other in silence. Klein's phone rings, and he doesn't answer it. Doesn't even flinch. Waiting for Roy to talk. It rings again, stops.

"Angela," says Roy eventually.

"Angela. She left, and you started having your problems again. Angela's the key. She's what came into your life. Made it better. Not the drugs. Her. And now she's gone."

"Angela," Roy repeats. "It's Angela."

"You fix that, and you fix yourself."

||||||||

IT TAKES Roy a few minutes to find the piece of paper amid the destruction of his kitchen. The phone lies shattered on the floor. The appliances are scattered, broken. The refrigerator door was left open, and the food inside stinks of rot. It was how he left the house when he headed out to the pharmacy. Wasn't in his right mind. Wasn't in his own mind.

He locates the number, the paper with the kittens on it. Tries out the living-room phone. A non-smashed phone. The answering machine is blinking. One message. He pushes the play button, hopes to hear her voice.

"Hey, buddy." It's Frankie. Low-key. "The other night . . . things got outta hand. We'd been . . . it had been bad, you know? This shit happens sometimes. So . . . whatever, I'm sorry, okay? I didn't . . . whatever. 'Case you wanna get in on something, I got some more scores lined up. Easy stuff, nothing too . . . well, if you want to talk, call me. I'm here. Anyway, gimme a call, whatever you wanna do. I'm here."

Roy erases the message. Glad Frankie called. Glad he apologized. Roy should do the same. But not now. He's got Angela's cell phone number in front of him. Can't call Frankie now. It will wait.

Roy dials. Waits for the connection. He hopes Angela has it turned on. He doesn't like leaving messages. A message means he's been recorded. Captured. Anyone can play it back, hear it, use his voice however they like. Worse still, what if her phone's lying around the house, and Heather picks up? He might hang up, in that case. Might end it all with a hang-up.

" 'Lo?" A man's voice. Roy looks down at the paper in his hand. At the phone. He's pretty sure he dialed the right number.

"Hello," says Roy. "Maybe I got the wrong number, here. . . ."

"Maybe you do." A gruff voice. Not a friendly voice.

"I'm looking for Angela."

"What?"

"For Angela. This is her—Roy. Tell her it's Roy."

"Oh. Yeah." There's a pause. He can hear a TV blaring in the background. Music, incoherent sounds. "Yeah, hold on."

Yelling, muted. The guy's hand on the phone, Roy thinks. Calling something out. A yell back, a shouted conversation. A crash. Something falling. Roy stands up, paces the living room, cord tangling around his legs. There's nothing on the line now. Did the guy hang up? Does he have to call back?

"Hello?" It's Angela.

"Angie, it's Roy."

"Hey! Hey, I tried to call you!"

"Yeah? I was out. Who was that?"

"Who?"

"Before, the guy on the phone."

"That? That was Joe." She drops her volume to a whisper. "He's an asshole."

"Your mom's boyfriend?"

"Yeah. She lets him stay over. Don't worry about Joe, he's just drunk."

In the background, Roy can hear more banging, more yelling. Something else crashing to the floor. That man shouting, screaming away. Not a place for a kid to be. Not a place for Angela. "He drink a lot?"

"Yeah," says Angela. "He can put it away sometimes—" She stops, and Roy hears the sound of a scuffle. "Get the fuck off me, Joe," she mutters. "And don't answer my fucking phone." Roy can hear the exertion in her voice. Like she's pushing him away. Pushing him off her.

"You need me to come up there?"

"No," Angela says quickly. "I can take care of him." She shifts gears, back to her usual perky self. "I'm glad you called. When can I come back down?"

"I was thinking Saturday. Maybe we'll take a trip—"

"I can come tomorrow, if you want. I've got school off."

"No, I got . . . business to take care of tomorrow."

"Ooh, I can help."

"Not that kind of business. You'll come down on Saturday, okay?"

A pause. Upset? Pouting? "I'll take the eight-thirty train. We'll have fun, I swear it."

Roy untangles himself from the phone cord, sits down in his recliner. "Good, then. It's settled."

"Settled."

There's a pause. Roy tries to listen for Joe, for that drunken lunatic. Can't hear him. "We gonna sit on the phone for a while?" Angela says eventually. "I mean, I got a lotta free minutes . . ."

"See you Saturday," laughs Roy.

"Saturday. Bye, Dad."

Roy gets in his own parting words this time. "Bye, Angie."

He hangs up the phone and sits for a while. Stares down at the carpet. Wonders if he should call back. If he should tell her what he's planning on doing tomorrow afternoon. If he should clue her in on everything, let her be part of the plan.

Better to wait. Better to surprise her with it. Better to see if it's possible first before bringing it up. But he needs to set up the meeting. See if he can work it out for tomorrow afternoon. Before Angela arrives.

One more phone call. Roy lifts the phone again and dials Information. This isn't a number he knows by heart, and he's glad for that.

THIS MAN Glasser is dressed better than Roy is, even with the new suit from the mall. The fabric is better, Roy is sure. The cut is better. The tie isn't as bold, as garish. He's understated, but classy. It's not just the suit, though. It's the leather furniture. The burnished wood. Even the paint on the walls. Roy doesn't often feel intimidated. In here, he's not on solid ground. In here, he's not comfortable.

The man can tell. "Is the chair fitting you?" he asks. "I can have Sandra bring in a different one."

"It's fine," says Roy. Doesn't want to be a bother. He fidgets with the paperweights on the man's desk. Heavy. Odd. Pictures of the man's children line the walls of the office. Vacation photos. Graduation snapshots. A wife, here and there.

"So what're we looking at, Mr. Glasser?" Roy asks. "This a hard thing to do?"

Papers on the desk. Roy's papers, all of them. The man shuffles them around, glasses perched on the end of his nose. "It's never easy," he says. "It's always a strain, especially if there's pull from the other side."

"There might be."

"Then that's an added problem we should account for." The attorney pushes his glasses back toward his face, secures them tight around his ears. "But to start with, the court is going to want to see an income."

"Money, I got. That's not a problem."

"I understand that. But they're going to want to see something . . . verifiable. A job. A career. Do you have one of those?"

Roy shakes his head. "Not so we can tell the judge, no. I got fronts, but . . ."

Glasser nods. "I understand. That's item number one to fix up. Along with that, I can't seem to find any of your income tax statements over the last few years."

"I got statements. Self-employed. Antiques dealer. Fronts again."

"Mm-hmm. You'll want to bring those in, then. We can look at them together."

"I can do that. I got that down."

Mr. Glasser sits back in his chair. Rubs the bridge of his nose. Looking up at the ceiling, not at Roy. "Stable home environment?"

"Yeah, sure. I guess."

"No arrests? No drugs?"

"No, no," Roy says quickly. "Nothing like that."

"Good. Character witnesses?"

Roy shrugs. "Again, not so many you'd wanna bring in front of a judge. Unless you count my shrink."

The attorney shakes his head, comes upright in the chair. "Let's not mention the therapy if we can avoid it. You get an old judge, they can be skittish about that sort of thing. Tell me: How does the girl's mother feel about this?"

"She won't talk to me."

"So you haven't discussed it."

Roy squirms more in the chair. "I'm telling you she won't even speak to me, how're we gonna have a discussion?"

Glasser backs off. "Hey, I'm on your side here. Just trying to get all the ducks in a row."

Roy understands. But he's not comfortable with all the questions. With all the maneuvers. "Tell me straight," says Roy. He wants the truth. Needs to hear an answer one way or the other. "I got a shot at this?"

The glasses are off now. Elbows on the desk. "I've handled cases like yours before. Lots of them worse. Each one different. It depends on the judge and on the day and sometimes I still think they make their decisions based on the shape of the moon. But it's not unheard of that you should get joint custody of your daughter. If everything comes out the way we'd like, you very well might.

"But we've got a lot to work on before filing anything with the courts. To be more specific, you've got a lot to work on. I don't like to go in front of a judge with my hands half-tied behind my back. I don't want to have to say that you're *going* to get a job and that you're *going* to show community involvement. I want to have that track record going back at least a few months from the moment we step into that courtroom. In short, you've got to be willing to change your lifestyle—your house, your car, your means of employment—everything—in order to get joint custody of that little girl. If that's what you want, then that's what you need to do.

"So you tell me, before we go any further with this: Are you prepared to do that?"

|||||||||

ROY DOESN'T tell Angela where they're going, and she doesn't figure it out until they're already well inside the parking lot. In the distance, past the entrance booths, she can make out the top half of the towering Ferris wheel. Smell the corn dogs. Hear the music.

"But you hate carnivals," she says to Roy.

He shrugs. "Never been to one with you. Maybe I just haven't seen 'em right."

Angela laughs and grabs Roy's hand, pulling him through the parking lot, toward the main gates. She's got on overalls today, and Roy can't help but think they make her look younger. More vulnerable. More in need of his protection. She's just a little girl, after all.

"If they've got it here, you're gonna love this one roller coaster," Angela begins, "with a double loop, and then it comes down into this twisty thing—"

"Whoa, whoa, we're gonna have to see about roller coasters."

"Oh, don't be a baby," she chides.

"I got a real nervous stomach."

"You'll love it. I promise." She stops in the parking lot. Turns. Catches his eye. "Trust me, okay?"

Roy nods. Realizes a second later that he means it.

The line at the ticket booth is short; business hasn't picked up yet for the day. Angela and Roy quickly make their way to the front, where an older woman waits to take their money. She's sixty, easy, hair bleached, a charm necklace hanging out of her sweatshirt. A ready smile for Angela when she approaches the booth.

"One adult and one student," Angela says. Roy gave her money in the parking lot so she could feel like she was treating him. Taking him out for the day.

The cashier rings it up. "That's twenty-one fifty, darling."

Angela reaches into her pocket and pulls out two twenty-dollar bills. "That's funny," she says. "All I've got is twenties. I thought I had some change around here. . . ."

"No problem, dear," says the older woman. "I've got all the change you need right back here."

Roy looks down. Realizes exactly what she's doing. He grabs her shoulder, squeezes, and Angela looks up. Mischievous grin on that face. Sparkle in those eyes. Roy shakes his head. She nods back. He shakes it again, and Angela turns away, back to the cashier.

The woman pushes the carnival tickets toward Angela and passes her the correct change. "Y'all have a great time at the fair," she says, and prepares to go on to the next customer.

But Angela's not budging. "That's a great necklace," she says, leaning in.

The woman beams. "Thank you, honey—my grandkids got it for me." She points to the charms dangling from the thin gold rope. "Each one of these is another one of my babies. Three boys, two girls."

"Gosh," says Angela, "that's amazing. Five grandchildren . . ."

"And another on the way. I get any more, and I won't be able to keep my neck up."

Angela laughs along with the woman, and starts to move away. Roy's glad. It's what he was hoping for.

But she stops a moment later, her hand digging into her pocket. "Oh, wait a second. I think I found some change."

That's it. She's running the twenties on this old lady at the carnival. Roy grabs her wrist, gently but purposefully. Pulling her away. "No, you didn't." Turns to the cashier. "She didn't."

"I did," Angela insists. "I found a dollar fifty—"

"No. You didn't. Not today. Okay? Not today."

Angela looks up at Roy, her eyes narrowing. Head cocked. Trying to figure him out. He doesn't say another word. Doesn't need to. Just looks back, hoping that they can get through this without a scene. "You're right," she says eventually. "I didn't." And she lets Roy lead her into the park.

"Okay," she says once they're inside, "what was that all about?"

"I didn't want to start off that way."

"You're not making sense."

They fall into a large group of people heading toward the midway. "The thing is," says Roy, "I'd like to see if we can get through the day without running any games."

"At all?"

"At all."

"Why?" she asks. "It's fun."

"Sure it's fun, but it's . . . it's not what fathers and . . . their daughters do. Together. It's not done."

"So what? We're different."

"We are. And I like that. But . . . Look, can we just do this? You and me? Try to make it through the whole, entire day without playing the con? No grift, nothing?"

"I guess," Angela says. "If that's what you want."

"That's what I want."

Roy sticks out his palm, and Angela stares at it. Not upset. Thinking it over. He smiles down at her, opens his hand wider, and she takes it. Grins. Enthusiasm back in her voice, her body, her motions.

"C'mon," she says, pulling him off into the heart of the carnival. "I know a great ride we can throw up on."

||||||||

THE DAY passes in a seemingly endless stream of loops and twists, rolls and shivers. Roy can't believe that he's making himself nauseated on purpose. But it doesn't result in vomit. It doesn't carry with it that stinging taste of bile. It doesn't have the head spins and the confusion. Nausea, in this manner, isn't all that bad. Roy can almost understand the thrill of the rides.

Angela doesn't seem to be affected by the same gravitational forces. She's not dizzy, she's not green. He wonders if she's from some other planet. Sent down to trick the humans into spinning themselves into a stupor. First wave of attack, incapacitating the native population.

For lunch, they have food on a stick. Roy nibbles on skewered meats; Angela eats anything fried. She has trouble balancing her tray of food along with the six stuffed animals Roy won at the game booths. Easy pickings, every one. Roy had worked the carny scene for a few months in the days before he met up with Hank. He knows the tricks, the ways to win. Hit the back corner of the bucket. Push out on the bottle instead of pulling up. That sort of thing. A prize for Angela every time. It's not quite fair, but Roy doesn't consider it running the grift. You can't con a con man.

"You got real lucky with that metabolism," Roy says as they sit on a splintered wood bench. The horse show is only a few hundred feet away, and when the wind shifts, it takes away Roy's appetite. He eats in shifts. "That stuff would kill most people on the spot."

"Yeah," mumbles Angela through the fried crust of her sugar-coated elephant ear. "I can eat almost anything."

"Your mom still like that? Thin as a pin?"

Angela shrugs. "She's normal, I guess. I don't do meals with her, so I dunno what she can eat anymore."

"No dinners at home?"

"Not really. I get something from the fridge and take it back to my room. Or I go out. Or she goes out."

"And Joe?"

Angela's eyes cloud over. "What about him?"

"What's he do?"

"I don't care. Forget about Joe."

Roy picks at the vegetables they sandwiched between his meat. Waste of space. "So how often do you see your mom?" Hopes he's not being too obvious.

"I dunno. I go to school, I come home, she's working. She comes home, I go out . . . A little bit every day, I guess. Half hour, whatever."

Half hour. That's the kind of thing he needs to tell the attorney. That's the kind of thing they can use in court.

"That's not a lot."

"Nope."

Roy laughs. Tries to make it casual. "Probably see me more than you do her."

"Yep."

"Angela," he says, putting his skewer on the plate. "We . . . we have fun, yeah?"

"We have a lotta fun. After lunch, I'm thinking we hit the spook houses. Most of 'em, they don't scare me, but I think I saw a walk-through back by the tilt-a-whirl."

"Okay. Okay, I'll try that." He shifts gears again. "And I'm . . . you think I'm okay . . . as a dad? You know, as . . ."

"I think you're great," she says, smiling up at him with genuine affection.

"Yeah?"

"Yeah. I was worried—you know, back at the beginning. 'Cause it was weird and all, and . . . and I didn't know you and you didn't know me. But now . . . now it's perfect, right?"

"Right," says Roy. "Right."

Angela goes back to her fried dough. Roy can't eat another bite. His stomach is all twisted. Heart pounding. After-effects from the rides. Must be. "Angela," he says, fighting past his quickly closing throat, "how would you like it if maybe I filed for joint custody?"

She stops eating. Puts down the food. "Of me?"

"No, of my six other daughters. Yeah, of you."

She thinks about it, just for a second. "So I could live with you?"

"Part-time."

"More than I do now?"

"Yeah, if you want. We can maybe find you a school down here, if you want. I don't know—I don't have all the details worked out yet."

"And mom couldn't complain about it?"

"She could complain, sure, but . . . I wanted to ask you first, before I went through with this. It's going to mean a lot of changes. Not between us, but . . . for me. For what I do, for how I work."

"And you'd do that?"

"Yes," says Roy. "I would. I will."

Angela nods. Scoots closer to Roy on the bench. Their legs are touching. "Okay. I'd like that a lot."

Five minutes later, they're done with lunch. Five minutes after that, Roy is fighting gravity on his way through the Rainbow Coaster. Stomach bottoming out, then slamming back into his throat. Legs tight against the restraints. Probably bruised. Somehow more nauseated than he already was. Angela grabbing his arm on the way down, screaming into his ear. Nearly deafening him, he thinks. Keeping up a steady shriek all throughout the ride. Eardrum close to shattered. He can't remember ever having a better time.

HE MEETS Frankie at a nice restaurant downtown because he doesn't want a scene. If they meet up in the diner, Roy knows, his partner will have no reservations about trashing the place. About yelling. About yelling at Roy. And though he might deserve it, though he might be betraying the friendship, the partnership, he doesn't want that. Can't have it, not with everything else on his plate and his mind.

Frankie shows up ten minutes late, wandering through the restaurant. His suit is crisp, stylish. Roy's surprised he knows what stylish is. Angela's fashion sense is rubbing off on him. Frankie cranes his neck, searching around. Roy stands, waves. Frankie streams through the crowd, weaves through the tables.

"Thanks for coming down," says Roy.

"No problem, man. It's good to see you." He puts out a tentative hand, and Roy grabs it. They shake, and pull each other into an awkward hug. It's all the apology either one needs. Frankie's shiner is fading, the black-and-blue streaks around his right eye turning pale once again.

"Sit, sit," says Roy. "I ordered you a vodka already."

Frankie pulls out a chair and spreads himself out. Shaking his head. "You're looking good. You lost more weight."

Roy shrugs. Knows he has. No fault of his own, but it's happened. "Up one week, down another." Eyes Frankie's clothes. "You going out tonight?"

Frankie snaps his lapels. "Rhonda."

"From the club?"

"The very same. You?"

Roy spreads his arms. "Dinner with you."

"You swinger, you." Frankie laughs. The waiter arrives with his vodka, and he throws back a gulp. "Nice place," he says. "So why are we here?"

Roy grins. " 'Cause we're fancy guys?"

"Nah, we're boondogs. You got another reason, partner. We gonna knock this place over together? Run some old-time con on them?"

Roy shakes his head, looks down at his bread plate. "That ain't . . . that ain't it, partner."

"Too bad. Some real money in here."

"Yeah. There probably is." Roy doesn't want to do this wrong. Doesn't want to limp his way through it. He raises his head, forces himself to meet Frankie's eyes. "I'm getting out."

"We just got here."

"I'm getting out of the life. I'm dropping the game."

Frankie doesn't say a word. Reaches for his drink, throws back the rest of it. Shakes the ice around, twirling it in the glass. Roy doesn't want to press it. Wants Frankie to talk first.

"You teaming up with someone else?"

"No—"

" 'Cause of what happened back at the station?"

"No, it's—I'm not teaming up with anyone else," says Roy. "I'm out. Gone. I'm gonna . . . hell, I don't know what I'm gonna do. Maybe I'll really sell antiques, I don't know. Work in a carpet store."

"A carpet store?"

"Whatever, I don't know. Point is, I'm getting out. I'm—I'm gonna try to get custody of Angela, and to do that, I've got to have some sort of normal life."

"A mark's life."

"Yeah," Roy says. "A mark's life. I gotta be the chump who gets taken on the street."

Frankie sits back, leaning against the stiff wooden chair. "And you'd do that for the girl? You'd switch sides like that?"

"That's what I'm doing." Roy looks around the restaurant. Gauges the distance to the other tables. If Frankie starts yelling, starts in on him, he's got to shut him up quickly. Keep it down, keep it calm.

"Well, then," says Frankie, leaning back in, "I wish you good luck."

Roy's forehead contracts. This doesn't sound right. "Serious?"

"Serious. What, I'm gonna stop you from having a family? I think you're a fucking moron, but that ain't nothing new." Frankie cracks a grin. It's infectious. "Hey, Roy—you been good to me for a lotta years. You taught me shit . . . man, I never woulda thought that stuff up myself. And if now you wanna get out, then I'm not gonna throw down and scream and yell."

"Good," says Roy, a bit stunned. "Good. I—I didn't know how you were gonna take it."

"Now you know."

"Right. Now I know."

They pick at the bread. Roy spreads a pat of butter along the side. "I do gotta ask you one favor, though," says Frankie.

"Anything." Roy's glad to oblige, relieved at what has been the easiest discussion he could have imagined.

"One more game to put me over the top."

"Frankie—"

"One more, just so I go out on my own with a little nest egg."

"I don't know. . . ."

Frankie puts down his bread, pulls his chair closer to Roy's. "If I gotta go out on my own, or—or if I gotta find myself a new partner—I'm gonna need a stash to hold me for a while. I can't pull it in by myself the way I pulled it in with you."

"You'll be fine."

"Eventually, sure. But it's gonna take me a while to get up to speed. We do one final game together, a good one, then I'll be set. I'll be set, and you won't have to worry about Frankie lying in the street somewhere."

Roy rubs his eyes, his forehead. This is a new feeling, one that's settling on him like a cloud. No pressure, no blurred vision. A vague uneasiness in the pit of his stomach. A sense that he should be helping, though he doesn't want to. Roy wonders if this is guilt. He wonders if this is what it feels like.

"I'm in a bad spot here, Frankie," he begins. "I gotta get myself turned around. I'm thinking cold turkey—"

"And I can help you. I can set you up with a legit job if you want. My cousin's got that furniture plant across town—maybe he can get you a supervisor's job or something, I dunno. All I'm asking for is one last score. We'll split it, like always. Go out on top, you and me."

"Go out on top . . ."

"That's what I'm saying. One last score. To close it out. A big ol' feather in your cap, Roy. That's what I'm talking about."

Roy doesn't want to commit, but knows that he will, eventually. "I gotta think this over."

Frankie nods and picks up his menu. "If you owe me anything, Roy, it's this one small thing."

TWO

IN THE three weeks it takes for Roy to set up the final game of his life, Angela comes and goes twice. Stays for five days at a stretch, bringing over some of her things each time. A bedspread here, a makeup kit there. The kind of things that make up a home. Roy doesn't say anything. Watches and smiles, that's all.

He knows he should call Heather, discuss the situation with her. Explain his motives. Reintroduce himself after all this time. But Angela says she's out most of the time, and when she's in, still isn't interested in talking to her ex-husband. Resentment. Anger. Inertia. He knows he'll be talking to her soon enough. Or her lawyer. In a few months, once all this is over, once this last game is played out straight, he'll have a real job. A real life he can point to. An employer, a salary. Maybe volunteer at the local shelter. Something, the lawyer said, to help his standing. To get him some good character witnesses. Then he'll file for joint custody, and the real game will start. He's sure Heather will speak to him then. He hopes she won't.

Saif was overjoyed when Roy and Frankie showed up at the warehouse. They'd come over late, after a scheduled art delivery. In anticipation of his new life, Roy had voluntarily cut himself out of the art deal, handing the future proceeds over to Frankie. "You are back," Saif crooned, hugging them both tight. "But our shipment has not come in yet."

"We're not here for the art," Roy said. He knew he needed to play this right. Didn't want to spook the Turk. "Frankie here . . . he's finally got me thinking you might be good with us. In our game."

"Your game. As . . . partners?"

Roy sighed. "Once. Partners once. Then, maybe later, you team up with Frankie here. If it goes well."

"And you?"

"I drop out. It's getting too much for me." He had no need to tell this guy about Angela. Not before he needed to know.

Saif was interested. Drooling, practically. "How do we do this?"

"The thing is," Frankie interrupted, "we need to know that you can make a score and play it right. And the only way to do that is to front yourself for the first game."

"I don't understand," said Saif. "Perhaps my English—"

"Your English is fine," Roy said. "What Frankie's saying is this: If you want in, you have to put up the advance dough for the first game. Way back, you told me you wanted to run long con—"

"Yes, yes—"

"—and long con requires capital. You want in with us—with Frankie—you gotta show that capital up top."

He took no time thinking it over. "I can do this," he said excitedly. "I can do this, certainly. And you two will provide the . . . game, yes?"

Frankie and Roy grinned at one another inside that warehouse. Big, toothy smiles. "Oh, we got a game," said Frankie. "We got a game, and we've got a beautiful mark waiting for the score."

That was a week ago. Since then, Roy's been trying to put himself together. Operating two lives. Talking to lawyers, to Klein, to real estate agents during the day. Setting up the grift at night. Speaking with the right people. Procuring the right goods. Roy's come up with a fun little twist, and Frankie put his own spin on the deal. It's a good one. Old school. Not quite long-con, not quite short-con, but it's the kind of thing that he'll miss.

"Mr. Arbeiter will see you now." Roy looks up, startled at the voice. The receptionist is talking to him. He puts down the magazine he wasn't reading and stands. Smooths out his slacks. Straightens his tie. He's never been on a job interview before.

"You look uncomfortable," says Arbeiter as Roy takes a seat in his office. "Would you like a drink of water?" The guy is younger than Roy, clearly. Wears his position easily.

Roy shakes his head. His palms are clammy, sweaty. The office has a large window in back, looking out over a parking lot. The walls are brick, unpainted. "I'm good," he says. "We can just get started."

Arbeiter asks some innocent questions. Age, interests. Leafs through Roy's résumé. Angela helped him type it up. Learned how in her Social Studies class at school. "No college degree?" he asks.

"No," says Roy. Wants to keep it simple. Doesn't want to slip. He put down that he graduated from high school. Didn't want to lie on the application, wanted a clean start, but Angela told him everyone does it. No one has a clean start. "I couldn't afford it."

The boss nods and flips the page. His hands look so young, Roy thinks. He can't be older than thirty, thirty-two. And he's the boss. "So you sold antiques."

Roy nods. "For a while, yes. Sir."

"That a hard thing to do?"

"Not hard to sell them. Hard to make a business of it."

Arbeiter leans back in his chair, hands folded across his chest. "We're not all born businessmen, Roy. Some men are better at it than others."

Roy doesn't know if he's being smug. Doesn't care. For a moment, he wants to leap across the desk. Grab this asshole by his tie. Tell him that he's beat the snot out of younger men, out of stronger men. Tell him he wouldn't stand a chance in the real world. Outside this office.

But that's old Roy. New Roy needs a job. A verifiable job, at least until he's got custody of Angela. After that . . . Well, there's always quitting time.

"I'd just like the opportunity to work in a good company," Roy says dutifully. The words sting his throat. He thinks about Angela. Steels himself. "If I can sell antiques, I can sell . . . what is it you make here?"

"Air-conditioning units."

"Air-conditioning units. Same principles of sale. You give me a chance, I'll sell a thousand of those things."

"I'm sure you will. Okay, thanks for coming in."

Roy remains seated. "I need—I need a job."

"Right. We'll call you."

Roy shakes his head. "I will work hard."

"Right," the boss repeats, his tone firm. "And we will call you. Thank you." He stands, and Roy takes this as his cue to leave. They shake hands, and Roy shuffles out. In the waiting room are five other applicants. They look up at him as he passes. Looking for a sign.

"Air-conditioning," he tells one skittish-looking woman in the far corner. "In case he asks, they sell air-conditioning."

||||||||||

THE NIGHT before the game is set to go down, Angela sleeps over. The room is pretty much hers by now. Roy shoved the ceramic horse into a far corner, took down all the paintings she didn't like. The horse only has walking-around cash in it now, ten thousand at the most. The watercolors went directly in the trash. Angela's got her own sense of style, her own sense of place. Roy knows she likes tulips. Bought some at the grocery store last time he went, put them in a vase next to her bed.

Roy watches as she brushes her hair, preparing for a good night's sleep. She knows what's going down tomorrow. Knows it on an intimate level. Despite his initial objections, Angela will be in on the game. It's the only way it will work right, the only way it can go down. There's other ways to play it, but this one works best. Hit 'em with the right connection, and you can take out any mark. That's what they need if this is going to work. That's what Frankie needs if he's going to be on his own.

Roy sits down on the edge of her bed. He's bought her a real, honest-to-goodness bed to replace the fold-out twin sofa. It's got a headboard and a footboard. Top-of-the-line mattress. She picked it out at the store. While she was doing that, Roy filled out an application. He could sell mattresses. No problem. "You feelin' good about tomorrow, kid?"

"Sure," she says. "What's not to feel good about?"

"Nothing. Just making sure you don't have the jitters."

"Jitter free, Daddy-O." She puts down the brush and climbs into bed, pulling her hair back into a ponytail. Securing it with a rubber band. "You can't do it without me, anyway. Right?"

"That's right. And what'd we discuss—if there's any problems—"

"If there are any problems, I run. I run to the train station and I get home to Mom."

"Good."

"But there won't be any problems," she says. "I know it."

"I know it, too. Now tuck in."

Angela climbs under her covers, drawing them up. Arranging her pillows just so. She pulls Roy over to her, draping his arm around her shoulders. He's halfway on the bed, his daughter tucked into his arm, leaning against his body. She snuggles in tighter. Staring up at Roy. "And when it's all over . . ."

This is a game they've been playing for weeks. "When it's all over," Roy says, "we'll . . . sell this place, and buy a big house in the country."

Angela's turn. "When it's all over . . . you'll have a great job working at a pet store."

"A pet store, huh?"

"Yep. There's perks, see. They let you bring home one dog a day, and all cats are half price."

"Good store. Okay. When it's all over . . . we'll have a pool with an inner tube slide and a ten-meter diving board."

"Ooh, that's good." Her eyelids drop, head sinking lower on the pillow. "When it's all over, we'll spend the summers together . . ."

"And the winters, if you want. We'll find you a good school, and you'll make some good friends, and we'll set you up right."

". . . and things'll patch up between you and mom . . ."

Roy is quiet. He's not playing the game anymore. Just listening. Knowing what she wants. That it won't happen.

". . . and then . . . we can all be . . . a family again."

Angela is asleep in his arms. At the very least, she's dreaming. Roy doesn't want to wake her up. Not yet. He gingerly pulls himself away, carefully catching her head as it falls. Laying it against the pillow. Wishing her a good night's sleep.

||||||||

THEY MEET on a darkened corner two blocks away from the theater. Angela, Roy, and Frankie pull up in one car; Saif comes by foot. He has the large gym bag Roy gave him for transporting the money. It hangs heavily off Saif's shoulder, weighing him down. Roy hopes Saif plays it like he thinks he will. It all depends on that.

"This is your daughter, then?" Saif asks, holding out his hands.

"This is Angela."

Saif leans down. "Your father is a very courageous man. A very good man."

"I know."

"To give up . . . all this. For you. You know that, yes?"

"Yeah, I know it." Angela looks up at Roy. Does this need to go on?

Roy reaches out for Saif's bag. "You brought the money?"

"All of it. It's quite heavy." He sets the gym bag on the ground and pulls back the zipper. Inside are stacks of hundred-dollar bills wrapped in cellophane. Bricks of cash. "Three hundred thousand dollars. The bait, yes?"

"What's the Saran Wrap for?" asks Frankie.

"I could not find the . . . the wrappers. You know? And I did not want to go into a bank and ask for a hundred ties."

"It's fine," says Roy. "Let's get moving."

Saif zips the gym bag back up and throws it over his shoulder. They emerge onto the street and head down the sidewalk, keeping in a tight formation. "This is very exciting to me," Saif says. "To begin this way."

"Excitement don't enter into it," says Roy. "You gotta treat this like any other job."

"Yes, of course, but—"

"No *but*. This is an exchange, that's what's got to go down. That's how it seems it should go down, at least. You don't think anything different, and it'll all go okay."

A block before the theater, they arrive at a small office building. Frankie pulls a key out of his pocket and works the lock. "You got everything you need?" Roy asks.

"It's all inside," says Frankie. "I'll change here, get over there quick, wait it out in the bathroom."

"Fine. Just make sure you pop when it's time."

"I always do." Frankie opens the door and steps inside. Reaches a hand back out, grabs Roy's. "This is it, partner. Last dance."

"Last dance," echoes Roy. "Play it safe, kid."

The door closes, and Frankie is inside the building. Saif, Roy, and Angela walk on. Saif leans into Roy, trying to balance the gym bag on his hip. "A question," he says. "How do we get the bag back once the . . . the mark has left?"

"We don't," says Roy. "No need." He's not being clear enough. "The thing is, if this goes down right, he won't have the bag. Frankie's gonna jump when the merchandise is on the floor, and—look, just let me do the talking in there, okay? Let me run the deal, and it's all gonna go fine."

Saif nods. "And this mark . . . he will fall for it?"

"He'll fall for it hard," Roy promises. "He's a dealer from outta town. I found him a while back, got his trust big. He won't suspect a thing, and we'll be home free. Like I said, we don't get involved with the drug trade—it's a rule. So you'll take the merchandise, sell it however it is you sell it, and distribute the cut. But you've gotta play it right."

Angela can't help but interrupt. "Roy says it's a classic blow-off."

"Right, hon. Old school."

Saif says, "Yes, it seems simple."

"It's never simple," corrects Roy. "It just comes off that way. It's set up tight, and nothing should go wrong. But if something happens—"

"Such as?"

"I don't know, that's the point. Anything. If it breaks down, you get yourself outta there fast. I can't protect you." He puts his arm around Angela, hugging her close. "Inside, she's my main concern, not you. If things go bad, I'm protecting her before anything else."

"As it should be," says Saif.

They round the corner. No one's on the street this time of night, especially down here. In front of them is the old Adelphi theater, long since abandoned. "Now, from everything we know, this guy should fall over easy, so the blow-off should stick. Inside, we keep to the new names we talked about. And after it's over, best thing to do is to skip town for a while."

"Maybe we can check out Fiji," Angela suggests. "I saw it in a magazine. Blue water, big mountains."

"Sure, hon. Fiji's great."

The walls of the Adelphi are covered in graffiti. Bright orange scrawls, yellow names scattered on the concrete. The windows are boarded up, the front door padlocked. Roy leads the group past the main entrance and into a back alley. Next to a side entrance door is another window, marked with a red Q. Roy reaches up and pulls hard at the boards. They come up as one, lifting on a set of recessed hinges. "Fake front. Go, file in."

Saif climbs inside, throwing the gym bag in front of him. Angela's next; Roy helps lift her into place. She winks as she passes through, and Roy winks back before following her inside.

Trash lines the floor of the abandoned theater. Plastic bags, food trays. Needles, beer bottles, used condoms. The screen of the once palatial movie house has been ripped into dangling shreds. Seats ripped out of their mooring. Foam cushions scattered along the floor.

"Guess they canceled the late show," says Angela.

Roy clears a path through the trash, kicking out at the rubbish. "They closed it up about ten years ago. Lotta deals go down in here."

"With you?"

Roy shrugs. "Yeah. Sometimes with me."

Saif lags behind them, muttering to himself. Roy can't make out what he's saying. "You coming?" he calls, and Saif smiles and nods. Picks up the pace.

Movement behind the shredded movie screen. A shadow. Roy puts out a hand, holding Angela back. "Mr. Thomas?" he calls out. "That you?"

There's stumbling, heavy footsteps tripping over unseen trash. "Too fucking dark back here." The silhouette, coming closer. Breaking into the light. A short, well-built man in a thin sweater stumbles out from behind the screen, stepping onto the narrow stage. Like Saif, he's also got himself a gym bag. "Nice place you got here."

Roy climbs up, pulling Angela with him. Saif does likewise. "Good to see you again," says Roy, shaking the man's hand.

"You're late."

"We're sorry about that."

"I don't like tardiness."

Roy shakes his head. "It couldn't be avoided."

"I had to pee," Angela says, just on cue.

The guy looks at the three of them. At Angela. "And this?"

"My daughter."

"You brought a kid?"

"She knows what's on."

Angela shoots a grin in the man's direction. "I been at it for years."

Mr. Thomas backs off. "You got your own family problems, I don't care. Look, we doing this or are we doing this?"

Roy motions for Saif to step up. The Turk takes his place.

"This is Alan," says Roy. "Friend of mine from way back. Alan, show the man the cash."

Saif plops the gym bag on the ground and theatrically unzips the top. The bricks are still there, wrapped up good and tight. "Three hundred thousand dollars," says Saif.

"The fuck is with the cellophane?"

Roy shoots Saif a look, fields the question himself. "Didn't have time to find wrappers. Money is money, who cares how it's wrapped? Let's see what you're bringing to the table."

Thomas doesn't press the matter. He throws his own bag to Roy, who staggers backward at the weight. Opens the top, letting Saif get a good look at what's inside.

Six plastic bags, each one stuffed with a pure white powder. Roy pokes one with a finger. Full, packed. Firm. "Nice," he says. "Better be pure—"

"Goddamned right it's pure," says Thomas defensively. "Send you so high—"

"Just asking," Roy says. "Just asking."

Thomas looks around, foot tapping impatiently. "So are we done here? We gonna trade goods?" He looks to Saif's gym bag.

"I'd say we're done."

"Good," says Angela. "Place gives me the creeps."

A crash, from up near where the lobby used to be. A crash and the sounds of scuffling. Of walking. Everyone freezes in place, Thomas's head darting from left to right. "Shhh," whispers Roy. "Stay still."

A beam of light flicks on behind the rows of seats; they can see it strobing back and forth. Coming closer to the theater itself. A man's voice, calling out, "Who's back there? Darryl, is that you again?"

No motion from the four on the stage. They wait in the shadows. Hiding in the darkness. Waiting for the light to pass them by.

"You can't be back here," says the voice. "I kicked you out last week, I'm gonna kick you out again. You want me to find you a shelter, I'll find you a shelter, but don't think I'm gonna waste my time running your ass downtown again."

The silhouette entering the theater is front-lit by his flashlight, but it's not hard to make out the uniform behind it. Brimmed cap, sharp lapels. Long shadow dangling off the right hip. It's a cop.

"Jesus Christ," he mutters, reaching for his pistol, fumbling with the holster snaps.

Thomas drops to one knee, reaching into his pants, pulling out his own gun, aiming it at the officer—

Who's already got the four of them dead to rights. "Drop it," screams the cop. "Drop the goddamned weapon." He advances on them, stepping over the trash as he walks down the aisle.

Thomas lets his weapon thunk to the ground. Roy's eyes blaze with anger. "Motherfucker," he says, pushing Thomas in the chest, throwing him to the ground, "you set us up!"

"What?" Thomas scoots backward along the ground, away from Roy's outstretched arms. "I don't know what—"

"I'll have you killed for this. Killed."

"Shut up, the both of you," says the cop. He steps onto the stage, flicking off the flashlight with one hand and tucking it back into his belt. With the light out of their eyes, the four of them can make out the officer's features now. It's Frankie.

"Hey," says Roy, "can't we make a deal here?"

Frankie aims his gun at Roy's chest. "I said shut up."

"Dad?" says Angela, looking toward Roy, laying it on thick.

"It's okay," he tells her. "Hang tight."

Frankie kneels down by the gym bag on the floor, keeping his gun trained on Thomas. Rips open one of the containers, letting some of the powder drip out. Sticks his finger into the mixture, licks it off. "Y'all a couple of big-time drug smugglers? Bringing a kid along, that's real smart. That'll look good in front of a judge."

Frankie pulls out a walkie-talkie and flicks it on. Static fills the empty air. "Base, I've got a possible four-thirty-three in progress," he says, cutting through the white noise. "Down at the old Adelphi theater on Sixth, gonna need two squads for backup."

Thomas takes a step forward. Staring at Frankie's gun, giving it a good once-over. Roy tries to motion him back, eyes wide. The guy doesn't listen, doesn't see. Roy shoots a worried look to Saif, who shrugs.

"I've got three suspects," Frankie continues. "One minor."

Another step forward. Thomas is smiling now, a full grin on his face. He takes another step forward, and another. Frankie raises the gun higher, tightening his grip. "Stay where you are. Right there, don't take another step."

Thomas doesn't listen. "For chrissakes," Roy yells, "quit it, it's over—"

But Thomas just laughs. He's not listening to Roy. He's not listening to Frankie. "I don't think so," he says. Reaching down, grabbing his own gun. Pointing it at Frankie, at Roy, at Saif. At Angela.

Saif has begun to sweat. He looks around helplessly. Hands working over themselves, rubbing together. Anxious. "Please," he begs, "this man is a police officer. He won't—"

"This man ain't crap," says Thomas.

Frankie looks to Roy. Roy nods. Frankie lifts the gun higher. "Drop the piece, or I'll shoot."

"With what?" asks Thomas. "Blanks? You're gonna shoot me with blanks?"

Frankie trembles. "I've got backup coming."

"You've got dick coming. Put down the gun. Or don't, I couldn't care." Thomas steps confidently into Frankie's line of fire, wrapping his hand around the barrel of the gun. Ripping it from his palm. Throwing it over his shoulder.

Angela runs to Roy, buries her head in his shoulder. He holds her close, arms around her body. Hugging her tight.

"You fucks were trying to screw me over," says Thomas. "You were trying to set me up."

"No, man," Roy counters. "I never met this pig before, I swear it."

Thomas isn't listening. "You think I never seen this before? You think we don't have bunco schemes back where I come from, huh? I've never seen the cop blow-off before?"

Frankie backs up. Still sticking to the script. "I don't know what you're talking about, but if you don't—"

Thomas slams the butt of his gun into Frankie's face. He goes down hard, hands clutched around his nose. Howling in pain.

"Big bad police officer comes in," Thomas continues, "makes a scene. Supposed to scare me off so I run outta here without my money. Without my dope. Nice trick. Nice try. Or maybe you got other friends on the outside who rush in as Chicken Little's 'backup' force. Arrest us, put us in fake squad cars. Knock me out, and I wake up with no bags, nothing. Maybe that was the plan?"

Thomas picks up both gym bags, slinging them over his

shoulders, and strolls up to Saif. His swarthy tones blanched of color. Mustache drooping. Breath coming fast. "So which one was it?" asks Thomas.

Saif shakes his head. "I don't know what you're talking about."

Thomas's hand lashes out, grabbing Saif by the jaw. Forcing it open, shoving the barrel of the gun inside. Thomas cocks the hammer. "I'll ask you once, and if I don't like the answer, I'll indicate it by pulling my finger against this trigger. So tell me: Was . . . that . . . the . . . plan?"

Saif nods, teeth rattling against metal. Nods again, and again, near tears. A high trill emanates from his throat. Thomas pulls the gun out of the Turk's mouth. "That was it," Saif admits. "The first one . . . the first one . . ."

"Jesus Christ," mutters Roy. "Nice going."

Thomas walks back to the middle, keeping them all under the gun. "Now, the question isn't how do I get rid of you, but which one of you do I kill first?"

"Take the money," says Frankie. "Take it, the money, the drugs. We won't say a thing. Swear."

But Thomas is shaking his head. Smiling. "That's no fun. I gotta have my fun, right? I could kill you first, of course. Fake cop. Not as much fun as a real one, but that's no matter." He points the gun back at Saif, who cowers. "And this one . . . who knows what this one will do when it all goes down. Might get to see him wet himself."

Thomas takes a step toward Roy and Angela. Pushes them apart with the barrel of the gun. Inspects Angela up and down. Nodding his approval. "And then there's this little one. What's your name?"

"Leave her alone," snarls Roy.

"Shut up, old man. What's your name, honey?"

She can barely get it out. "An—An—Angela."

Roy takes a step forward. "Goddamn it, I said leave her alone."

Thomas pays him no mind. Runs the barrel of the gun down Angela's shoulder, down and across her hip. "You're a pretty little thing, Angela. How would you like to come home with me?"

"I—no, I don't—"

"That's all right," Thomas says, smoothing out her hair. "We can do it right here."

Something animal, nonhuman. A growl, a trill. A roar through the air. Roy charges toward Thomas, his head down, bull-like. Arms spread wide to take him down, to knock him off his feet.

Frankie screams, "Roy—no—"

A deafening blast as the gun goes off. Acrid smoke fills the air, and Roy collapses to the ground, clutching his stomach. Blood seeps from between his fingers, pooling on the theater floor below.

Angela shrieks and runs to his side, falling on top of his body. "Daddy," she sobs. "Daddy . . ."

As Thomas approaches to grab Angela off her fallen father, Frankie jumps on the man from behind. Grabbing his arms, pinning them to his sides. The gym bags slamming into each other, twisting around into impromptu restraints. Thomas twists around, flailing about, and the two go down in a heap, falling to the stage. They struggle for the gun, each one trying to wrest control.

Saif doesn't know what to do. He stands there, shell-shocked. Staring at the scene. "Go!" Frankie screams. "Get outta here!"

Saif takes another look at the scene—at Roy, bleeding to death on the ground. At Angela, crying and screaming, trying to get her father to wake up. Frankie and Thomas rolling around, fighting to see who will get control of the gun. Saif doesn't wait around to find out. He leaps off the stage and sprints down the aisle, heading for the window and the street beyond.

The struggle continues for a few more minutes, their motions becoming less violent as the seconds pass. Soon, Frankie and Thomas stop wrestling altogether. They lie on the floor, panting. This was tough, fighting like this. Tougher than they'd expected.

"Knock it off," Frankie says, throwing Thomas off of him. "He's gone."

"You sure?"

"Yeah, yeah, he's gone. Halfway back to Turkey by now."

Thomas stands up and helps Frankie to his feet. "You almost took off my goddamn arm, you know that?"

"*Me?* You hit me with that gun any harder, and I'm up in the hospital for a broken nose."

Thomas shrugs. "Roy said make it look real, so I made it look real."

They turn to Roy, to Angela still sprawled over his bleeding body. She's not crying anymore. The grin on her face says it all. "I did good, huh?"

"Hate to admit it," says Frankie. "But you did all right, kid."

Roy opens his eyes. Stares up at the group. "Looked pretty good from down here. Help me up."

They drag Roy to his feet. His stomach is a mess of red liquid. "I set one of the squibs backward," he says, rubbing his belly. "Hurt like a motherfucker."

Frankie to Thomas, shaking his head. "And Marco, what's up with the baby powder?"

Thomas—Marco—grins abashedly. "I couldn't find any flour."

Roy laughs. "You know how hard it was not to make a face when I tasted that shit?"

" 'Least your lips'll be rash free." Marco shakes his head in amazement. "You see how fast that guy ran outta here? Like his ass was on fire."

"That's the plan," says Roy. "Let's get outta here. We'll divvy it up at home."

They hop off the stage and begin to make their way up the aisle, toward the main theater exit. Frankie throws an arm around Roy's shoulder. "I'm gonna miss you, man."

Roy nods. "You, too. But it was a good capper."

"Good times," says Frankie. "Way to go out."

Angela squirms her way in between them. Comfortable in the middle. "So we're set now, Roy?"

"We're set," he replies. Relieved, in a way. It's over. The last fifteen years, the games, the con. Done. His new life, whatever that means, can finally begin. "All the way."

They step into the lobby. Roy is surprised to hear voices. Slivers of light outside, through the cracks under the double doors. No one should be out there this time of night. No one should be anywhere near here.

Light explodes into the theater as the front doors blow wide open. A rush of voices, barking commands, yelling orders. Roy, falling backward, stumbling on his feet. Holding up his forearm to block out the light. Angela, grabbing on to him. Grasping his arm. Tight.

Saif steps into the theater, flanked by two uniformed officers. Real officers. Not Frankie's kind of cop. He's got a badge hanging around his neck. The mustache is gone. The accent is gone, too.

"See that belly wound healed up on you," says Saif. His speech is perfect, plain old American.

Roy's face twists into a mask of dread. This wasn't how it was supposed to go down. This wasn't how it was supposed to end.

Angela's fear is real now. Grasping at Roy, holding on to him. "What's going on—Roy, what's going on—"

He stumbles back again, away from Saif, away from the two other officers. Away from Saif's gun, out of the holster and pointed at them. He should have known. He should have pegged the guy from the start. Never should have even gone to the warehouse. Never should have brought him in on the deal.

"I knew you were rotten," Roy says plainly. "Day one, I knew it."

"Thanks for your trust . . . *partner,*" says Saif, stepping into the lobby. Keeping them at bay. "Scam in a scam. It's a good one. They don't run it anymore, but it's a good one. I'm glad I stuck around with you two."

Roy looks to the exits. Blocked off. The other two cops flank the group, one on either side. Roy backs up a little farther, Angela by his right. Terrified. He never should have brought her. Never should have involved her in this.

"Make for a good story in the papers," Saif continues. " 'Con and his cohort, Little Miss Mischief.' Hell, something like that."

Roy can feel the pressure coming on. Most days, he'd force it away. Think about something else. Now, he's egging it. Stroking it. Hoping it will grow. Bile in his throat. This was not his plan.

This was not how it was supposed to go down. They should be home by now. Counting the money. Ending this nonsense.

"You killed us, Frankie," Roy says plainly.

"Jesus, Roy," Frankie protests, his own voice trembling. "I didn't know. I thought—I thought he was clean."

"You killed us."

Saif lowers his gun for a moment, reaching behind him to pull out a set of handcuffs. Roy can't drag his eyes away. Handcuffs. He's never been in them. Doesn't think he'll enjoy the sensation. The pressure builds a little more. Vision blurring, not enough. He can't work up the anger. The rage. He knows he's beat. Those handcuffs, coming closer.

Next to him, Angela is staring at Saif's gun. It's not trained on them anymore. It's down. Down enough. Roy sees it all—her look, the gun, the thoughts going through her head.

It happens slowly. So slowly, Roy wonders why he's stiff, immobile, why he can't do anything about it. Roy can't help but watch as Angela crouches down, legs tucked beneath her, springing up, springing out. It's around then that Roy starts screaming, but it comes out late. Comes out long and loose instead of fast and sharp.

Angela's body is tight against Saif's, her fingers clawing into his flesh. Drawing blood, scratching at his face. Furrows scraping down his cheeks, huge red welts blistering the skin. Roy gets his feet moving, throwing himself at the struggling pair, trying to pull Angela off the cop. "You can't do it," he yells, "Stop it, Angela, stop it—"

Roy can sense the other cops coming up behind him. Sense their presence running to his side. Doesn't care. He tugs at Angela, trying to save her, trying to keep her from further harm. It's all over for him, for them as a pair. But not for her. It doesn't have to be all over for her. He can spin this right, he can play this for a judge—

Pain, exploding in his head. Not the right kind of pain. Not the pressure. Just a sharp, spreading ache. Out of his rapidly dimming vision, he can see one of the cops lift his baton again. Swirl it through the air. Bringing it down atop Roy's head.

A grunt. A soft wheeze of air. No pain this time. Just sensation. Movement. The theater picks itself up, flips on its side. Everything is crooked. Spun upside down. Roy's cheek hits the lobby floor, his body landing hard on its side. Head wobbling. Eyes dancing in their sockets.

The theater is dimming again. Roy wonders what's going on. Did they leave? Did they leave and close the door? He can see feet, groups of them, dancing back and forth on the ground. He can hear a commotion, still. What's going on? The lights are still fading.

There's a shot. A gunshot. Sharp, loud. Echoing. A gunshot and a scream. It's Angela. Angela is screaming. The lights are gone now, and Angela is screaming. Fading fast, but it's her.

Angela is screaming, Roy thinks one last time before passing out. *Angela is screaming, so I must have done something wrong. I take it back. I take it all back.*

ONE

LYING ON a beach, suit pulled down low beneath his stomach. Roy looks down, expecting to see flesh and hair. Surprised to find his belly mostly gone. Thin, tanned waistline. It's good to see. Been many years. The sun is bright today. Not hot, but bright. Can't really feel any heat off it, but that's no worry. It's bright, and that's all that matters.

Breeze from the east. Can't feel that, either, but it's carrying the sailboats along. Whipping the wind, throwing hats off parents' heads, making a mess of their kids' sand castles. Blue water, see-through. Fish swimming by the shore, multicolored fins and shining scales. Easy water.

Angela is one lounge chair over, sunning herself. A blue bikini he bought for her . . . somewhere. Somewhere up in the little town. They visited one of the local shops. Met the owner. He laughed with them, fed them orange soda. Sold them bathing trunks for Roy, a few necklaces made out of shells and shark's teeth. A blue bikini for Angela.

She looks over at Roy and smiles. She's older than Roy remembers. Older than she was when they bought her that suit, but that's no matter. She's a grown woman now. Beautiful. She's started dating already, and Roy doesn't mind. He tells her to be careful, he checks out the boys she's seeing, but so far he's approved. Can't remember any of them, but he knows he must have approved.

She's reading, too. Schoolwork, he thinks. Studying even while on vacation. She's a good girl. He's glad he won custody. Glad they could take this trip. Doesn't remember the middle parts, doesn't remember how they got here, but that's the lure of the islands. You can forget everything and just relax.

He waves. Smiles. She waves back. Only ten feet away, but there's no need for anything else. Just to know she's close by, resting. Comfortable. Content.

"Ya da da da dee," she says, smiling.

Roy doesn't understand her. He leans closer, grinning.

"Ya dee da da dee da." Insistent now. Like she needs him to understand.

But the surf is getting louder, and Roy can't make out what she's trying to say to him. He cups an ear.

"Ba dee da doo da dee dee dum," she repeats. "Ba da dee da dee doo. Da dee dee da da ba da la doo!" Calling over the waves. Raising her voice to be heard. Opening her mouth all the way, yelling it loud.

But he still can't make it out. What is she trying to say to him? He tries to lift himself off the lounge chair but finds that he can't. He's stuck there, lying on his side, cheek pressed into the taut fabric. Tries to pry himself off. Upright. He can't do it.

He looks up, to Angela. For help, for assistance. She's gone.

The lounge chair is empty, only the blue bikini top blowing in the breeze. She's not on the beach anymore. No one's on the beach anymore. The sand is turning black. The sky is turning black. But he can hear her calling out to him, singing those nonsense syllables, even as the lounge chair buckles and engulfs him, drawing him down, into the shore, into the surf.

||||||||

A TRUMPET, ya-da-da-ing up and down the scale. He can see it, a pair of little children, one boy and one girl, running back and forth, climbing a huge set of stairs, sliding back down the banister. The trumpet goes up, and the kids zoom past. The trumpet descends, and the kids slide on by. Images, floating past his mind. Through his mind. A bass now, thumping out the rhythm, a bouncing ball those kids are chasing. Bounce, thump, boom, thump. All going past him. Through him.

Bumps, not musical. Shaking his body, slamming his head against something not quite hard, not quite soft. Leather. Something leather. Each bump a warning jolt of pain. His head, pulsing. Pressure, external. Like a vise around his temples, squeezing.

Road noise. The sound of tires on pavement, of a car moving at considerable speed. He's lying on a leather seat. Two leather seats, sprawled out. Bucket seats. Black leather bucket seats. Frankie's car.

The trumpet. The music and the car. Frankie's here. He's in the back of Frankie's car. Can't imagine why. Can't figure out why his head hurts like it does. And isn't someone else supposed to be with him? A . . . a woman?

Roy props his hands on the seat and tries to push himself up. No strength in his arms. No motion. Tries to turn over, to call out Frankie's name. His mouth's not working. Drool spills out one side, puddling under his cheek.

He needs to lift his head. To lift his head and find Frankie. To ask him what's going on, what's happening. Roy steels himself, readies the muscles in his neck. Lifts. His head comes up, floating in the air, and Roy thinks that this isn't so bad, this wasn't so hard to do.

Another bright bolt of pain, a flash of light before his eyes, and he's down again, face mashed into leather. Blue skies and warm sand. Back on the beach, in Fiji. Back on the beach with Angela.

ROLLING ALONG again, faceup. He's able to open his eyes. For a second, no more. The light, blinding. Carving into his head. Discussion around him. Frankie's voice, somewhere, talking up a storm. Explaining something.

Left eyelid pulled open. A face above his, an unfamiliar face. Left eyelid closed. Right eyelid pulled open. That same face. He can see the body. Wearing green. Others wearing white.

More rolling. Bumping. He's being wheeled somewhere. Announcements over a public address system. Fuzzy. Loud. Crashing through, another bump. He tries to sit up, but can't. Straps around his head, he thinks. Around his arm, his body.

He tries to break free. Unable to do so. They're holding him down, he thinks. Holding him back. Trying to keep him from . . . from someone. That's the plan. They're trying to keep him down.

A jab in his arm. A prick, then it's gone. A sensation, building through his body. Glowing. Heaviness. Warmth.

WHEN ROY wakes, it is with the full knowledge that he's been unconscious. That he's been out of it for some time. He remembers the theater and he remembers the scam. He remembers that Saif turned out to be a cop, that it all went horribly wrong. He remembers that Angela got away from him. He remembers the gunshot and her screams. He just doesn't know where he is *now.*

Frankie's voice. He's nearby. "What do these lights mean?" he can hear him asking.

Another voice, female. Stern. Not Angela. "Please don't—sir, please don't touch that, it's sensitive equipment."

"They show if he's gonna wake up soon?" asks Frankie. "Like if—like when he's gonna wake up?"

"It's very expensive. Please, sir."

Roy opens his eyes. Bright, but not too bad. Not stabbing at his corneas like before. Clean white ceiling. Clean white linens. He grunts, trying to lift his head up.

Frankie's face suddenly looms overhead, taking up most of his vision. Out of proportion, out of focus. Large looming teeth, eyes bulging out. But it's Frankie. "Hey!" he cries, nearly shouting into Roy's face. "Hey, I think he's waking up." Frankie kneels down by the bed, by Roy's head. "You with us, buddy?"

Roy tries to nod. Barely moves his head. A nurse comes trotting over, notices Roy's movement. "I'll get the doctor," she says, and scurries out of the room. Frankie follows, closing the door behind her. He walks back to the bed.

"Roy, man, I was worried about you."

Roy wants to put it all together. Get all the information, figure it out on his own. But he's tired. Even though he just woke up, he still feels so tired. Concentrates on forming a sentence. Concentrates on forming a single word. "Where . . . ?"

"Tapper General Hospital," says Frankie. Roy doesn't know where that is. He's never heard of Tapper General in his life. "Didn't want to take you to the local bins, 'cause they'll be looking for you there. I drove for about two hundred miles, man. . . . You started to get all pale on me, and I got worried, so I figured this was far enough. You been out for like two days."

Two hundred miles in the backseat of Frankie's car. The germs back there. Roy can't think about it. He tries to sit up again, but the pain lances out with every effort. Frankie rests a hand on his chest. It feels leaden.

"You stay down," Frankie says. "They said you gotta stay lying down. This here's a private facility, and I got you in a real nice room. Good doctors, I think. I told 'em you were in a bar fight, and got hit over the head with a two-by-four. I think they went for it."

Roy doesn't care what Frankie told them. He needs to know the situation, the layout. He needs to know about Angela. Tries another word. "Wh . . . what . . . happened?"

Frankie's face twists in disgust. "I fucked up, that's what happened. That Saif, man . . . Two years I known him, can you believe that? Two years, and he winds up being a goddamned cop. I've seen more shit go down with that guy than half the pimps on the street, and *he's* the one busting us."

"No. What happened . . . after?"

"After? Hell, it wasn't pretty. Those other two cops started whacking you on the head, Marco took off running. I woulda split, too, but when I saw them beating on you like that . . . man, I just—I snapped, you know? Threw myself on one of 'em, starting whipping the tar outta him—"

"Angela—"

Frankie turns away. "And he was a strong motherfucker. Biceps like . . . fucking big biceps, man. But I got in a nice one under the jaw—"

Roy's hand shoots out from under his body. Grabbing Frankie by the lapel, pulling him close. All his strength in that arm, in that hand. "Angela," Roy says. Spittle drenches Frankie's face. "What happened to Angela?"

Frankie tries to turn away; it's no use. "They got her." Frankie sighs. "The cops, they got her."

The strength ebbs out of Roy's body. His arm falls off Frankie's jacket, dangling limp at his side. Eyelids close. Blot out the room. "It was a fucking mess in there," Frankie continues. "They had more cops out front, waiting. I had to get you out the back, sneak out through the shadows."

Roy's trying to think. Trying to remember the name of his lawyer. Wondering if he does criminal work. If he can help with this thing. "She—she didn't do anything," Roy says. "I can testify to that."

"Roy, no—"

"I'll give myself up. I'll give myself up, and I'll tell them I dragged her along. That she didn't have anything to do with it. That she was—"

"Roy," Frankie interrupts, "that's not it. It's not . . ." He stops, takes a breath. "She killed a cop, Roy."

"What?"

"She killed a cop. She killed Saif."

Roy's eyes are shut hard now, balled up tight. Squeezing out the world. "No—you got something mixed up, here. . . ."

"They were struggling," Frankie explains, each word a new blast into Roy's chest. "Her and Saif, for the gun. She had one hand on it, and—I guess there were shots. There was a shot. And he fell over. That's when the other cops broke out and . . . that's when it all broke down."

"No. No." He doesn't want to hear it. Can't hear it. Sounds of the surf. Sounds of the beach.

"She shot a cop, Roy. That's the bottom line. She didn't mean to, but . . . it's done."

Roy steels himself. Needs to be clear-headed. Needs to think. "Where is she?"

"County," says Frankie. "I made some calls, had some friends check up on her."

"Juvie ward?"

Frankie shakes his head. "They got her in adult lockup. Transferring her to the prison tomorrow."

Roy can remember the last time she was locked up. How she was still traumatized by it two hours later, outside the police station. She's fourteen. No place for a fourteen-year-old. She'll die in there. She'll be killed in there.

"Did you bail her out? She can't—she can't be in there."

Frankie shakes his head. "I don't have that kinda dough, man. The cops got the gym bag."

"How much is bail?"

"She killed a cop, man."

"How much?"

"Half a mil," says Frankie, his voice low. "Judge set it this morning. I'm sorry."

Roy's breath is long. Labored. There has to be a way to handle this. "What about Dominic?" Their bail bondsman friend is always at the ready, just in case.

"No can do," says Frankie. "Dom's outta town, and Eddie's not taking that kind of action when the boss man's away."

"Jackie?"

"I tried—he won't take it." Frankie pulls over a chair, sits next to Roy. "No bondsman's gonna take the bet. She killed a cop, she's a minor—that's a flight risk. They won't put it up, 'cause we don't have the collateral. I wish I had the cash, man. . . ."

"I've got it," says Roy. Decision made.

"What?"

"The cash. I've got the cash."

"Are you serious?"

Roy nods. It doesn't hurt quite as much this time. "Yeah, I can do it." He tries to sit up again, tries to right himself. Straining his atrophied abs, trying for a sit-up. Head crushing all the way, room going dark. Closing in from the corners. He collapses back on the bed. No use. Roy isn't going anywhere for a while.

"You gotta do it," Roy tells Frankie. "You gotta get her out."

"Me? I can't—I—if I walk into that station, I'm a dead man."

"Then get Dr. Klein to do it, anyone. I'll tell you where the money is, how to get it out, and you send a proxy in to spring her, okay?" His eyes stare up at Frankie. Pleading with him. "You do this for me."

"Okay," Frankie says. "Okay, I'll do it."

Roy lets out a long breath of air. The monitors beep away in the background. "There's an account at the Grand National Bank in the Caymans." He gives Frankie the fourteen-digit account number. Makes him memorize it. Repeat it back to him a few times. "When they ask for the password, you tell them it's Anafranil. Say it."

"Anafranil."

"Right. Have them transfer the half million to Klein's account here in the States. They'll put up a fuss, but insist on it. Get her out of there, fast. If you can come back to see me, do it. If not, hole her up somewhere."

Frankie grabs Roy's hand, holds it tight. "We're gonna get through this," he says. "We're gonna be fine, partner."

"Yeah," Roy says. A bitter laugh escapes his lips. "We're gonna be swell, huh?"

The door swings open a few moments later, and the nurse steps inside, followed by a steady stream of doctors. Frankie places Roy's hand back on the bed, slaps the doctors across the back, wishes them all good luck, and walks out of the room. At the doorway, he turns around one last time, to say good-bye. But he can't see Roy anymore. All he can make out is a small, prone figure surrounded by a curtain of white robes and plastic tubes.

||||||||

TWO DAYS pass, and Roy hasn't heard from anyone. Hasn't gotten a phone call, a visit. Nothing. Starting to worry that something went wrong. That Frankie got himself picked up. He tried to make an outgoing call this morning, tried Frankie's place, but the number kept ringing. Machine picked up, but he didn't want to leave a message in case the cops were listening in.

Klein's answering service was useless. Roy hung up before they even started talking. He'd dealt with them before. Didn't want to do it again.

A concussion, the doctors said. A major one, but nothing broken. Nothing that requires surgery. Rest and relaxation, no future bumps on the noggin. They said his brain swelled from the hits, that it caused enough pressure to knock him out for forty-eight hours. Said they'd seen worse, but usually it resulted in a coma. They were glad he came out of it all right, they said. Roy just laughed, and they ordered more tests.

The concussion isn't his concern anymore. Angela is. She's been on his mind the past two days, jolting him awake when he should be sleeping. Thinking about her in prison. With the other inmates. Crying herself to sleep. Wondering why she'd been abandoned. He needs to know what's happened to her. To Frankie, too, but mostly to Angela.

Roy hits the call button. He's been avoiding its use, trying to save it for emergencies. As he expected, the nurse comes quickly.

"Is something wrong?"

"Did anyone come by while I was sleeping?"

"I don't think so."

"Little girl, about fourteen? Hair down to here. Skinny guy, sunken eyeballs?"

The nurse shrugs. "I was on duty the whole time, but . . . I don't think you had any visitors. I'm sorry."

"She's my daughter. She was getting out of—she was supposed to come by. To see me."

The nurse nods knowingly. "It happens. People get busy."

"No, I—okay. Okay." He looks around the room, at his clothes hung over a chair. At the open bathroom door. He sits up in the bed, wincing with the effort. But it's not that bad. It's bearable. "What about phone calls? Did I get any phone calls?"

The nurse points to the beige push-button on the stand next to the bed. "Your phone's right there. Private rooms get private calls. If it didn't ring, you didn't get a call."

"Right," says Roy. "Right, but maybe I was sleeping, and the call got routed back to the front desk."

"We don't take messages."

"But maybe someone did. People do things sometimes, if you ask them nicely." Roy softens his tone. Asks nicely. "Could you check for me, please? If there are any messages?"

She sighs, huffs. About to refuse, but stops. "Be right back." Walks out of Roy's room, down the hallway, and up to the front desk.

"Nicole," she says, strutting up to the desk clerk, "you get any messages for the guy in 218?"

"Honey, you know we don't take messages. I look like an answering service to you?"

"That's what I told him."

"Then tell him again."

The nurse shuffles back down the hall, toward Roy's room. She opens the door and pokes her head through. "Like I said," she begins, "we don't take any—"

The room is empty. The bed is made. The linens are pulled up tight. The lights are off, and the chart is gone. Like no one was ever in there. Cleaned and ready for the next ailing customer.

||||||||

THE TAXI ride back into town is an expensive one, but Roy got lucky. His money clip was still in the pants he wore to the theater. To the hospital. A hundred and fifty dollars later, he's still got around eighty on him. Enough for fares around town. Doesn't want to go back to the house and pick up his car. Not yet. Not until he knows if they're looking for him.

The cab pulls up outside Frankie's apartment building. The green glass windows stare down at Roy, reflecting the sun. Blinding him. He tells the cabbie to wait outside. The driver doesn't mind. It's the best fare he's had in weeks.

Apartment 618, Roy remembers that much. There's a buzzer at the front door to the building, and he finds Frankie's name listed among the residents. Punches the code on a keypad. Waits for an answer.

Ringing. Like before, when he tried to call. Frankie's voice mail answers, and Roy hangs up. Not sure what to do. Sometimes Frankie doesn't answer the phone. Maybe he's lying low.

A resident comes down the elevator, making his way through the lobby. Roy watches him through the glass. Pretends he's talking into the monitor. "So you want me to come up?" Roy says loudly. "Gonna have to buzz me in." The man doesn't even see Roy, doesn't care about him. He leaves the building, the front door swinging wide. "I'll be up in a second," Roy calls, slipping inside the lobby and walking briskly to the elevator bank.

Sixth floor, and it doesn't take Roy long to find apartment 618. He recognizes the building layout now, remembers it well. This is definitely Frankie's place. He rings the doorbell and waits. The chimes echo inside the apartment, but he can't hear any scuffling about.

A bang on the door. His fist pounding the wood in rapid succession. "Frankie," he calls, trying to will his voice through the wood. "Frankie, it's me. Open up in there." Roy looks down at the carpet, at the swirling pattern. Wonders if he can see a smudge down there. If it's stained at all.

Another knock, another bang, Roy's knuckles rapping hard. "C'mon, Frankie," Roy yells, letting his voice carry. "Open the goddamned door if you're in there."

A tap on Roy's shoulder. Images flash through his mind—Frankie, Angela, sure, but mostly it's the police, on stakeout. Finding him here. Lucking out. Ready to take him away. It's over.

Shoulders slumped, Roy turns. Expecting to see a boy in blue. Instead, there's a little old man, four foot ten if he's an inch. Blue leisure suit, belt too wide. Toupee that doesn't quite match the remaining natural hair. "You looking for the guy who used to live there?"

"Yeah," says Roy. "Yeah, I . . ." Wait a second. "Used to?"

"Moved out yesterday. Made a mess of the whole place. Dragging boxes through the carpet . . . I've got a mind to call him up in front of the homeowner's board."

Roy shakes his head. "Wait, wait—he moved out?"

"With that daughter of his. Pretty girl. Foul mouth."

The daughter. Angela. Frankie must have sprung Angela from jail and gone into hiding. Good. This is good. "About fourteen," Roy says, "longish hair?"

The man shrugs. "I don't cotton much to the young girls anymore, but that sounds right."

Roy is already halfway down the hall. Gaining speed, heading for the elevator. He's got to find them, and he knows who will know where they are. "Thanks," he calls back to the old guy. "Thanks a lot."

He's not appeased. "You tell your friend he's got a lot of explaining to do. You tell him he'll have to explain himself when this is all over!"

THE DRIVE over to Dr. Klein's office is a slow one. A traffic jam has snarled the city streets, and the cabbie won't stop talking about his dream of owning an Orange Julius franchise. Roy sits in back. Thinking. Trying not to. Staring out the window, and trying to keep his mind blank.

By the time they get to Klein's, it's nearing five o'clock, and Roy is praying that the doctor is still in. Once again, he tells the cabbie to wait, promises an extra twenty. He's running out of cash, but there's still a bunch of bills left in the horse at home. If he can get back to his house after this, he can pay what he owes. If not, he'll borrow or blow the guy off. Either way works.

Roy waits by the elevator for two minutes before realizing it's out. Broken. He even sees the sign next to the call button. Hits the nearest stairwell and starts running. Four flights up, and by the third he's panting hard. Has to take the last one at a slow walk, pushing his body up each step.

Klein's office is at the end of the hall. Roy starts to pick up speed, staring at his watch. He's just in time. Klein won't be leaving for another fifteen minutes, at least. He'll get this figured out soon enough.

Roy grabs the door handle and pushes, his body colliding with the door a moment later. Odd. He turns the handle hard, pushes again, but the door refuses to open. Is it stuck? Throws his shoulder into it. No use.

Locked, then? Are they gone for the day? Roy pounds on the door, calls out to whoever might be inside, but there's no answer. This doesn't make sense.

He backs up a step, trying to figure this out. The door looks different. It's the right office, but the door is . . . changed, somehow. Same as it was before, Roy thinks, but . . . bigger. Taller.

Roy figures it out. It's not taller at all. There's just no nameplate on the outside. No gold square with Dr. Klein's name emblazoned on it. No gold there at all.

Instead, there's just a single sheet of paper, taped to the door. White all around, with bright red lettering. He's surprised he didn't see it before. Didn't want to see it before. Doesn't want to see it now.

Office for Lease, it reads. *See Building Manager.*

THE STREET is quiet, nearly empty. A kid on a ten-speed rides by and shoots Roy a nasty look. He doesn't even notice. He stands in the middle of the road, staring at the piece of paper in his hands. The letters and numbers blur in and out. Roy has had a lot to drink. On the piece of paper is an address, an address that matches the house in front of him. A smallish, yellow ranch home. Bars on the windows. But the lawn is kept up, the roof is solid.

Roy doesn't want to ring the bell, but he has no choice. If he wants to find her, he has no choice. He knows what's going to happen if he rings that bell. Once the door is answered. He doesn't want to recognize that fact. Not just yet. So he waits a little longer.

Fifteen minutes later, he's still standing in the middle of the road, still staring down at that paper. Staring at the house. The door opens.

A woman walks out, dressed in a simple T-shirt and cotton pants. She's thin, almost too thin, and her hair is up in a tight ponytail. It's been nearly fifteen years since Roy has seen her, but he recognizes her right away. Thinks for a moment about running off, but stands his ground.

"You want something?" she calls out. Coming closer, but keeping a path open back to her house. In case the guy should jump. In case he's a freak. "Or are you gonna stare at my house all day?"

"Hello," says Roy. His voice is scratchy. Doesn't sound like himself. He doesn't think it will make a difference.

"Hello," she says back.

"Hello, Heather."

He knows her name. Heather takes another step closer, and recognition begins to seep in. "Roy? Jesus . . . Roy?"

He nods. Stares down at the paper again. "I got your address. You were in the phone book." She's right across from him now. Standing on the sidewalk. He's still out in the street. "The whole time, you were in the phone book."

"Sure," she says. "Why not?"

He nods. "Why not."

They stand there. Heather is about to invite him inside when he speaks again.

"Have you seen her today?"

"Who?"

"Angela."

"Did I see . . . Roy, are you okay?"

"Something . . . bad happened. With Angela."

She shakes her head and takes another step toward him. As if she's going to take his arm. Lead him inside. "You want some coffee? I can make coffee."

"Angela," Roy repeats. "I think something happened to her, and I thought—I figured maybe she came here before . . . going off."

"I don't know who you're talking about."

"Angela!" Roy spits, stumbling backward, shaking off Heather's hand. "Our daughter. I'm talking about our daughter." Why can't she get this?

There's a long pause. Roy is hoping that his ex-wife is gathering her wits. Preparing to talk rationally. "I don't know what you're on right now. And I don't know why you're doing this. If you want to come inside—"

"Heather, please," Roy pleads. Near tears. First time in his life, and he's near tears. "Don't do this. We need to talk about our daughter—"

"We don't have a daughter!" she yelps. The words loud in Roy's ear. Piercing.

" 'Course we do—Angela. She's been coming to my place every few weeks, hanging out—"

"We don't have a kid, Roy." Heather's growing angrier with every passing moment. Working up a head of steam. "You and me, we don't have a daughter. Never did."

Roy shakes his head. The street spins, that nice yellow house suddenly tilting on its axis. "You left, you were pregnant—"

"Stop—"

"—you had her without me. She's our *daughter*—our Angela—"

"Stop it, Roy—"

"—she's our little girl, and—"

"I had the abortion, okay, Roy? Is that why you show up here after fifteen years, to find out what happened? I had the god-damned abortion!"

Silence from Roy's end. He stares blankly across the street. At the little yellow house. At the green lawn. At the solid roof.

"We never had a daughter," Heather continues, her voice lower now, softer, as she heads back toward the house. "And we never will. Good-bye, Roy." She pauses for a moment, then adds, "Don't come by again."

She steps into the house. Roy stands in the middle of the street. Looks at the numbers on his sheet of paper. They match the house in front of him. This is Heather's house. This is where Angela is supposed to be.

||||||||

AN HOUR later, in his den. Back resting against the edge of what was once Angela's bed. Phone in one hand, bottle of rum in the other. Cuts all along his feet, his legs. He doesn't care. He doesn't feel the pain. He stares out across the den. At the remains of the ceramic horse, smashed into a million pieces. Everything inside is gone. Staring at nothing. At the blank wall. Staring at the blank wall. This is where he wants to stay. This is how he wants to stay. How it should end. This is how it must have been planned from the start, from the first leg of the game. So easy to piece together. So hard to think about it.

He makes the final phone call, knowing what will happen. Knowing what the outcome is before he hears it. He's played the game enough to know what's gone on. He's been a master trickster, and as a master trickster, he knows when he's been tricked. But it's too late. He knows it too late.

They answer at the Grand Cayman National Bank, and when they do, Roy gives them his account number. He gives them his password. He waits while they access his account. Waits while they give him the balance. Waits while they tell him there's nothing left. Waits while they ask him if there's anything else they can do for him today. Waits as they ask again, as they call out to him. As they ask him if everything is all right. If he's still on the line. From far away, calling out to him, in the distance. Like he's on a ship, sailing off, and the rest of the world is left at port. Drifting off, a solo cruise, nothing else surrounding him. On his way to nowhere, everything and everyone left behind. Just a raft and blue waters and endless ocean as it all fades over the horizon.

ZERO

ROY WALKS into the diner and takes a seat at the counter. He doesn't know how long it's been since he's come here. Days, maybe. Weeks. The counter is filthy, grime coating the edges. He finds a seat that's less dirty than the others. Sits down. Tries to make himself comfortable. There's not much room up there, on that stool. Not much room to get situated.

The waitress walks over. "Where's your friend?" she asks.

"I don't know."

A nod. No further interrogation. "Turkey on rye?" she guesses, and Roy shrugs. Sounds right. The waitress walks away.

It's empty in the diner tonight. That's the way it goes some days. Full one hour, empty the next. Roy remembers that from the old days. The way people used to flow in and out. The way he would size them up. The way he and Frankie would watch them eat. Watch them move.

There's a conversation to his right, muted speech. Whispers. Roy doesn't focus on it, but it's not hard to make out. A couple of college kids, laughing. Giggling. They're getting more frequent in here. Roy wonders if he should choose a new place to eat.

"So I got a new trick to show you," one of them says loudly. "I got a new game."

"Please," says the other one, just as loud. As obvious. "You and card tricks. . . ."

Roy closes his eyes. He can smell the food in back, frying. He can feel the dirt beneath his feet, the ground-in grime on the diner floor. Hear the clink of dishes, the chatter of patrons. Taste the oil saturating the air.

"No, no," says the first kid. "This'll be great. I got this one down good."

There's a tap on Roy's shoulder. A presence to his right. He opens his eyes. Turns. There's one of the kids, brown hair and sweatshirt. Grinning. "Hey, mister," he says. "You wanna see my friend mess up a card trick?"

Roy takes a breath. Looks at the two of them. They can't stop smiling. Like they've already pulled the trick. Like they've already got the cash in their pockets. "Sure," says Roy. "I'll see a trick."

They introduce themselves as Bob and Dan, and go through the motions. "Pick a card," Dan says, "and don't show it to me." Roy slides a card out of the deck. It's a joker. "Okay, now put it back, anywhere. Good. Good."

As Dan shuffles, Roy lets his mind go. He wonders if Frankie's playing this game right now. Wonders if Angela—or whatever her real name happens to be—is playing the straight man. Wonders if they're pulling it off better than these two stiff college kids. He knows they are. Knows they can pull off anything.

"Right," says Dan, fingers fumbling with the deck. "Now I'm

gonna flip over some cards, here, and . . . and I'm gonna find your card, mister." He awkwardly starts throwing cards onto the table, faceup. Soon, the joker pops up, and Roy catches Bob giving his friend a big wink. It's a lousy signal, a blind man could see it coming, but Roy doesn't let on.

"See," says Bob, late on his cue. "You suck at these."

"No, no, wait, wait." Dan pauses. Thinks. "Betcha the next card I take off—I mean, the next card I flip over—*flip over*—I bet that's your card."

Bob digs into his pocket and takes out a ten-dollar bill. Slaps it on the table. "I'm in on that," he says. Turns to Roy, his eyes closed once again. "Mister? Mister?" Roy comes back. Looks at the joker lying there. Ready for the game to be closed. For the final pinch. "You wanna get in on this, mister?"

Roy nods. He stands, reaching into his pockets. Pulling out the bills inside. The quarters. The dimes. The pennies. All of it. A hospital ID tag, receipts from dinners with Angela. Everything. Into his jacket pockets, finding a few dollars there. Pushing the cash into a pile, shoving it into the middle of the table. Forty-seven dollars. All the money Roy has left in the world.

The college boys look at one another and shrug. "Time for magic," says Dan. "I said the next card I flip over'll be your card, right? Voila!" He clumsily flips the joker face-side down, and he and Bob erupt into a fit of laughter. Roy sits at the counter, nodding his head. A touch of a smile at the corners of his lips.

Dan slides the money into his wallet, and Bob slaps Roy on the back. "That was a good one," he says. "You gotta admit, mister, that's a pretty damn good one."

"It was. It was."

"No hard feelings?"

"No hard feelings."

Bob and Dan continue to congratulate themselves, ordering up dessert and a new round of sodas. Roy turns back to the counter and waits for his turkey on rye to arrive. He's got no way to pay for it now. It doesn't bother him. It might bother the waitress, but it doesn't bother him.

"You gotta watch yourself, mister," Dan calls out to him, still celebrating his triumph. "Friendly word of advice, you know? You can't trust everyone these days."

"Yeah," says his friend. "Next time, you gotta be careful. Next time, it won't just be a card game, I bet."

Roy doesn't answer. His turkey will be coming soon, and then he will eat. After that, he doesn't know what will happen. It's been a while since he's felt that way. Not knowing. Not planning. But he will eat, and he will drink his coffee, and that will be that. Something will come to him. Something to do. Some way to do it. This is his diner, after all. This is as good a place to start as any.

ACKNOWLEDGMENTS

This is the point in the book when I get to thank all those people who have helped along the way. Like an awards acceptance speech, it has the potential to drag on way too long; unlike an awards acceptance speech, you can always turn the page. Perhaps, then, I should keep this brief:

Thanks to Barbara Zitwer, all-around fabulous literary agent and doll baby, who bulldogs when she needs to bulldog and keeps my ego properly inflated.

Thanks to Jon Karp, editor extraordinaire, who lines his punches with velvet and makes sure I stay true to what I want to do.

Thanks to Brian Lipson, living proof that Hollywood agents can still have bite without being sharks.

Thanks to Jack Rapke, who clicked with this book—all of it—and knows how to make good material even better.

Thanks to Manny and Judi Garcia, my parents, for not disowning me after I lampooned them in my first book, and for always supporting my creative efforts since childhood.

Thanks to Howard and Beverly Erickson, for allowing me to marry their daughter, and for having faith in me when I was but a young, brash kid with stars in his eyes.

Thanks to Nathaniel Spiner for being the biggest *Matchstick Men* booster south of the sixth grade; if we grab the elementary school market, I owe it all to him. Thanks, as well, to his family—Noah, Blanche, Cheryl, and Eitan—for their constant excitement over all my projects.

And, of course, eternal thanks to my beautiful wife and daughter, Sabrina and Bailey, for making every moment of every day brighter than I ever could have imagined. Sabrina is the one for whom I write every word, and Bailey is my heart wrapped up in a giggling two-year-old body.

ABOUT THE AUTHOR

ERIC GARCIA grew up in Miami, Florida, and attended Cornell University and the University of Southern California, where he majored in creative writing and film. He lives outside Los Angeles with his wife, daughter, and dachshund, and is currently at work on *Hot and Sweaty Rex,* the third novel in his acclaimed series featuring dinosaur detective Vincent Rubio. He can be reached via the Internet at www.ericgarcia.com.